D1525128

CHARLIE COSSACK'S BAR AND GRILL

(Flash Fiction and Tales of Contrition)

GABRIEL GOLOVKIN

CHARLIE COSSACK'S BAR AND GRILL

DEDICATION

For Mary Regis, my partner in crime, and my one true love.

CHARLIE COSSACK'S BAR AND GRILL

CONTENTS

CHARLIE COSSACK'S BAR AND GRILL

ACKNOWLEDGEMENTS

I would like to thank all of you who became part of the story through my last work, "The White Cardinal." Out of the original tranche of print copies released, a total of one hundred of them have been passed on to readers throughout the United States and foreign countries. This data has been supplied to me by you, the reader. I find your tales of discovering the book and moving it forward to another reader fascinating as well as inspiring. To date, copies have been located in Australia, Sri Lanka, Moldova, and Belize.

Much is owed to your originality in passing this work on. Copies have been left at train, bus, and airport terminals, doctor's offices, and most forms of public transportation. At this time, "The White Cardinal" is off the shelf and unavailable electronically. It was truly time to put this to bed, but if you are still in possession of a print copy, please feel free to pass it on. I have heard some rumblings that electronic versions may become NFTs, but I am woefully ignorant of that process, so have at it.

Some of you tucked a crisp, new dollar bill between the pages as a bookmark and an indicator this was a "pass it on" work. Thank you for that, but I am not suggesting you should spend extra money in this process, your work in moving the book forward was in itself, all I could ask for.

So, after reading what you now hold in your hands, move it forward to a new reader, someone else who wants to become part of the story. Coffee shops, bistros, book stores, libraries, and your neighborhood book exchanges are just some of the possibilities, but I urge you to be aware of your decisions, we wouldn't want this work to be considered a nuisance and tossed into the trash, discarded as garbage, and not shared for its true purpose of storytelling.

Again, my deepest gratitude to those who became part of the story through "The White Cardinal," and to those who will pass this work on as well.   Whether you purchase it, or find it, keep moving it on, and let me know how you did so, whether it was done surreptitiously, or by simply leaving it on your friend's dining room table, I'd love to include your story in an upcoming work.

gabgolov@gmail.com

CHARLIE COSSACK'S BAR AND GRILL

I AM THAT LITTLE HEADACHE

You know me well. I am that little headache that comes and goes. I am that sensation that runs through your neck and brain. I am with you when you open that bottle of aspirin at the kitchen sink and when your thoughts begin to fade as you lay in bed.

We've met so many times in so many places. I am that slight tinge of fear, that slight disorientation so often dismissed as déjà-vu. I am that face in the crowd, that face so unremarkable, but yet so memorable. That face you pass on the street as you hurry to your next destination. I am that knock on the door heard only by you.

We have known each other for so many years, yet you choose to forget. More comfortable to vanquish me than to face the bizarre reality of our introduction. I have been the observer, the voyeur, for I have tunneled into your dreams. We have sat at your mother's kitchen table and shared a coffee, I have built fortresses for you and lowered drawbridge after drawbridge, yet you choose to forget.

I have shown you visions of joy and glory, grief and compassion, along with evil and avarice, yet you choose not to remember, you let these visions fade as night drifts into morning. But lately I have sensed a change, a change almost unnoticeable, but a change gaining momentum.

For now it is I who feel the headache of your presence, the anxiety surging from my shoulders, through my brain and eyes. It is now you who appears momentarily in the crowd, it is now you who brings the dizziness, the creeping fear of a voyeur.

When I wake suddenly in the silence of the night, it is your shadow at the foot of my bed. I find myself in front of a door, a large door, an oaken door, a door locked and bolted, and I hear you pounding your fists upon it. I press my hands against the door and feel the vibration of each dull thud. The hinges begin to pull from the jamb, dust and splinters fall onto the marble floor, but I am motionless, I am paralyzed, for at last, you have found me.

A CYNIC'S GUIDE TO SPONTANEOUS HUMAN COMBUSTION

UTICA, NY
1987

Hannigan Butler had been advised of the incident at Upstate Skilled Nursing through the Bishop's office. These requests came more often than people realized, investigating miracles and the circumstances surrounding them. The Bishop's office would call, just an aide, not the Bishop, and the clock would start ticking. Hannigan had debunked each and every one he had investigated over the past five years, and for the most part, each diocese was happy with that.

Usually zealots, interpreting unusual, but perfectly explainable incidents as miracles, and the locals all trying to make a buck or two from it. Hannigan often felt remorse after debunking an occurrence, a sense of guilt for snatching hope away from the few banking on that miracle cure, robbing them of the only thing they had left to hang on to. Once hope is gone life can become unbearable, but the hoaxers and zealots had already robbed them of their dignity, and that was comparatively worse in Hannigan's mind.

Before leaving, Hannigan called his sponsor, he needed to have a plan. He would need the availability of an AA meeting in Utica in case things started to spiral. He had been fighting a losing battle with alcoholism and drug addiction for the past decade. He would never win the war, so his only goal now was to stay functional as long as possible before another 27 day at a rehab center, or death. It was all so predictable yet unavoidable. Usually a woman, angry and over-sexed from her own substance abuse, swimming in denial, pushing the limits, just one drink which turns into a black-out binge, just one line of cocaine, but it's never just one line. He often wondered how long before his heart would simply explode or the jaundice would return, never to leave, but those worries faded fast when he was in the grips.

"St. Miriam's Hospital, every Wednesday at eight o'clock."

Jim was a walking encyclopedia when it came to AA meetings and locations. He'd been sober for twenty years after multiple lock-ups for DWI offenses and two failed marriages due to his alcoholism. He found a way to beat it and he thrived on helping others down that path.

"Thanks Jim. This is a weird one, a white cardinal appearing at a patient's room on and off, and then the patient goes up in smoke, the locals are blaming it on spontaneous human combustion."

"Sounds more like arson to me, so why is this being called a miracle?"

"It appears people who saw the bird formed a prayer group, and they say there's been some cures, but they always say that when someone goes into remission."

"Well, good luck Hannigan, if you need anything just give a call."

"Thanks Jim, I'm feeling more confident as of late, so hopefully I won't have to."

A lie, but why give Jim anything to worry about until it happens again, and inevitably it will, another setback in a long string of setbacks.

Hannigan hung the phone up, grabbed his suitcase along with a travel mug of coffee and once again embarked upon a pilgrimage to question faith and the basic principles of humanity. Just once, just once, he thought, I'd like to experience an actual miracle. The x-rays proving the cancer is gone, someone rolling out of their deathbed and going for a jog, trapped miners being led out of a collapse by an angel, just once, just fucking once.

The bad thing about driving any distance is the "thinking" time it involves. The would haves, the could haves, and the should haves. Hannigan had been an agent for the U.S. Treasury Department until the booze got the better of him. He was involved in some high level cases, including a counterfeiting ring with international ties. The phony money was so good it was detectable to only a few agents with specialized training and experience. Hannigan was one of them. After losing that job he acquired a private investigator's license and spent most of his time tracking cheating husbands and fraudsters. He was good with the fraud stuff. After one such case involving a faith healer, his investigation was profiled in a magazine with nation-wide circulation. That's how the Catholic Church found out about him. They were looking for a buffer between the parish priest and the congregation, a non-believer, a skeptic in the worst sense, someone who could deliver the cold, hard facts in a concise, scientific format.

"We still have parishioners believing you can gain fortune with God by burying a small statue of St. Joseph in your front yard, and in some cases it has to be buried upside down."

A frustrated parish priest had shared that with Hannigan.

"Sounds more like voodoo than Catholicism."

"You're exactly correct Mr. Butler," the priest continued, "but I can't tell them that, you need to."

The Bishop's aide had given Hannigan a list of contacts in regards to the incident at the nursing facility. Firefighters, police, nursing staff, and some believers claiming miracle cures and divine intervention. He'd need to get a look at the autopsy photos, and the room where it happened. Number one on the list would be the Fire Marshal's Office, they had yet to release a cause for the fire. Most likely why the rumors were still churning.

Hannigan was greeted by Captain Noah Gregory at the Marshal's office. The office was housed on the second floor of a working engine company. The engine was screaming out of the station when Hannigan pulled into the parking lot.

"Sounds like someone is having a bad day."

Hannigan shook Noah's hand before they ascended the steps,

diesel fumes permeated the atmosphere.

"That's the bad thing about this job, you meet some really nice people who are experiencing some really terrible things."

Noah seated himself at his desk, Hannigan was seated directly across from him. On the desk laid a manila folder, labeled with the name Alvin Bean and the skilled nursing facility's address. Noah flipped it open and slid it across the table to Hannigan.

"This isn't really all that unusual, to find someone bed-bound burned to death. Usually they've been sneaking a cigarette, they fall asleep, the cigarette ignites the oxygen tubing and the bed springs serve as a grill top, they're usually overweight so the fat melts off them like a pork roast, feeding the fire, sorry to be so crude about it."

"He was in a coma, right?"

"Yeah, that's why we're looking at the motor in the bed as a possible ignition source. We sent it to the State Police Lab, we're waiting on them now."

Hannigan leafed through the investigation photos. Nothing left but ash and fragments of some larger bones and the skull, yet no real damage to the room outside of soot on the wall and the ceiling immediately above.

"No smoke detectors?"

"Believe it or not, they're not required by code to be in the rooms, although we recommend it. The fire died out before the smoke reached the hallway detectors. The door was half open along with the window so the draft pulled the smoke away, or so it seems."

"Who was the last one in the room, if the motor isn't the cause, somebody set this guy on fire."

"A custodian. He used to sit with Alvin and say the Rosary, he knew him from years ago. He's an older guy, real nice guy, everybody loves him there."

"Think he'd talk to me?"

"Probably, his name is on the preliminary, I'll give you a copy."

"Can you give me directions to St. Miriam's Hospital, think I'm starting a sinus infection, saw a sign for them on the way in, thought I could get an antibiotic."

"Sure, no problem, the urgent care center closes at seven."

So what's it going to be, a bar or the AA meeting. A drink, just one drink would feel great after the drive. Hannigan would probably invest another two or three days here unless the lab report came back early about the motor.

He checked into his motel room, opened the curtains, and as luck would have it, there was a bar directly across the street. He watched the comings and goings. It was a busy place, and right next door was a liquor store. This could be heaven, this could be hell, better get to that meeting.

Hannigan arrived early to the meeting, lots of chairs set up, not many attendees yet. He'd have to introduce himself, he always hated that. He grabbed a cup of coffee, too strong as usual, and had a seat. Someone seated themselves next to him, he didn't like that, he liked space, he didn't like being elbow to elbow. He turned to catch a glimpse of his new neighbor.

"Well, Captain Gregory, funny meeting you here."

DAY DRINKING AT CHARLIE COSSACK'S

CHARLIE COSSACK'S BAR & GRILL
****
∎∎
HOME OF THE SPAGHETTI SANDWICH
AND
DAILY DRAFT BEER SPECIALS
***
HOURS
SUNDAY THRU SATURDAY
IF THE LIGHTS ARE ON WE'RE OPEN
∎∎

**
ENTER AT YOUR OWN PERIL
*
DO NOT FEED THE ANIMALS

UTICA, NY
1987

Hail, hail, the gang's all here. And they are quite a sight. Day drinking and smoking their way into another universe, an alternate reality, escapism for the common man.

Little Ricky Mankiller and his wife Melissa are slowly pouring beer into the feeding bag of her brother Merlin. They watch intently as the liquid courses from the bag into the clear tubing, flowing into his belly through his nose. He smiles and emits a loud, wet burp as the golden nectar reaches its destination. Stage IV pancreatic cancer I'm told, I just hope he doesn't die seated at the bar.

And in strolls Alvin Bean, right on time. Today he's sporting a military beret, and that could spell trouble, but today Alvin is beaming ear to ear. He shouldn't be drinking with the amount and types of medications he's on, but what the fuck, he's still the Alvin I knew as a kid, and I'll credit him with one thing, his delusions and fantasies are never self centered, they're all about making the world a better place.

Gennady enjoys the company of these human wrecks, he bartends through the blue haze created by his customers and dumps their ashtrays as necessary. Alvin loads his pipe with his favorite cherry tobacco and strikes a wooden match between his thumb and forefinger as if he is a magician.

Bohdan is escorting a Fire Marshal through the building on a public assembly inspection. He'll slip the Marshal a fifty and he'll forget anything he's seen here today. Day drinking used to be reserved for the third shift factory workers who lived in a parallel time zone, a time zone where breakfast is dinner and night life begins at 8:00 AM, but the economy is bad and the factories are all closed now, nonetheless, bar hours remain the same. Why mess with tradition.

I've just popped out of my office to grab a cup of coffee, and I can't help but admire the black eye Little Ricky has on display. It's a rainbow of colors and his eye is completely shut. Must have been quite a disagreement at the Mankiller homestead last night, and as usual, Ricky is worse for wear. Melissa is a big woman, and at times, a very mean drunk.

Gennady allows his favorites to carry a tab, but they're always advised they are indebted to me, whether it's for a drink or a loan, and they know when I come calling the debt is repaid in any fashion I choose. I own some insurance agencies throughout the state, or at least I own the identities of the individuals who do. Making claims through these pseudo-businesses has proved very profitable and an excellent means to launder money. Slip and falls, rear end collisions, and did you know household flooding results in just as many claims as fires?

I have a brigade of phony claimants, ranging from the dancers at my clubs to the desperate gamblers and drunks frequenting my bar, willing and able to cough up their settlements to me as long as I cover premiums and slip them a few bucks when they are in need. In some cases, involving legitimate clients, I never submit their premiums to parent companies, I simply pocket them and pay any real claims myself. What a web I have weaved – doctors, chiropractors, pharmacists, traffic cops, ambulance chasing lawyers, and insurance adjustors, all validating the bogus claims my cadre submits. In a few instances, I created identities out of whole cloth to file claims on life insurance policies. A corrupt ER physician and a funeral director or two, convinced they aren't harming anyone. Five copies of the death certificate and I go to town. How insanely simple it has all become, and it all gets kicked up the ladder to me.

Keep filling those prescriptions for pain killers, I'll remarket them in short order, that auto body shop – I own it, and please don't miss a visit to the chiropractor, he owes me as well. I have even submitted claims against a couple of my strip clubs – six inch heels to blame of course. It's all just so crazy stupid I'm having trouble shuffling the money from pile to pile. The best part, however, is my employer in Toronto has no idea of the scope of fraud I have created. For every dollar I give him, I'm keeping three for myself.

"Hey Charlie, Bonita says she's running late, probably a half hour or so."

Gennady gently hangs up the phone and pours Little Ricky another draft beer.

Bonita Romero is a bankruptcy attorney and has orchestrated most of my flow chart of fraud. My employer connected me with her a year or so ago when he realized I was excavating a mountain of money in upstate New York. Initially, she established shell companies and off shore accounts, sucking out any assets of legitimate businesses through mergers before running them into the ground, but as of late she has created a maze of money laundering through my insurance businesses and strip clubs. And what I find most mind-boggling is that I actually have legitimate investments as well.

We're meeting today to develop an escape clause, because, as we all know, when something is too good to be true, it is definitely too good to be true. Unfortunately, Bonita has taken an interest in me romantically, and I fear it may hamper decision making on her part. She's also a sloppy drinker and a single mother who is hell bent on punishing her ex-husband. I need to keep her sober and focused for my own well being. To that extent, I'll tell her anything she wants to hear.

Bohdan doesn't care for her. He makes no secret of it. "Bonita Romero, sound like porn star or stripper, stupid name." She doesn't like him either, noting his grubby appearance to me on many occasions.

Before returning to my office, I motion Gennady to come towards me. "Hey, why don't you give Little Ricky some ice for that shiner, it looks horrible."

"Sure boss, she's going to wind up killing that poor bastard."

Alvin stands at attention, dons a pair of goggles and salutes Gennady, who enthusiastically returns the salute. His bicycle and a garbage bag full of cans are propped adjacent to the front door and he is no doubt on his way to the recycling center. Depending on how much he gets, he'll either return or spend the rest of the day scavenging for more treasure throughout city parks and storefronts.

But today, day drinking at my bar takes an unexpected turn. Alvin pulls his bicycle into traffic, the bag of cans on his shoulder obstructing his vision, and he is struck by a vehicle. As the fire engine and ambulance arrive, Alvin is bleeding profusely from his head, his arms are drawn into his chest, and Gennady is motioning bystanders to step away. A patrol car has blocked access to the street and an officer is consoling the driver of the vehicle, an elderly woman who is experiencing the worst day of her long life.

The ambulance pulls away, but the impact has left the street strewn with cans and broken bottles, along with Alvin's unlaced tennis shoes. Looking back, in all the years I have known him, I can't recall a single occasion in which Alvin laced any pair of shoes he was wearing. Most often the laces were missing, but if they still existed they were untied and filthy from street wear. Might be a little too late to ask him why now, but if he pulls through, he's going to need a new bicycle. I'll walk him down to Sears and have him pick one out, any one he wants, probably one with high handle bars and a banana seat, that would be his style. I just hope he can still ride it.

AIR RAID

ST. ANTHONY'S ACADEMY
1962

The three of us trudged behind Mr. DiFabio. Alvin was desperately trying to grab Mr. D's pants leg as Charlie Cossack hop-stepped to keep up with them. I lagged behind, worrying about my upcoming reaction to the thing the three of us feared most. The air raid siren, that demon mounted on the wall, put there to warn us of destruction and imminent death.

Alvin summed it up best one day. "If we're all going to die anyway, why hide under our desks?"

Sister Mary Bridget didn't reply, probably because there was no good answer. She kept the three of us in her classroom during lunch hour to discuss the events of the past week. We got to eat lunch at our desks, but it came with a price.

We all loved her, the sweet Irish brogue, a wicked sense of humor, that beautiful complexion peeking out from her habit. I may have loved her more than the rest, habit or no habit, she was my Marilyn Monroe. Once in a while, to liven things up, she would lift Alvin from his desk and tuck him under her arm, moving through the aisles as if she was carrying a football to the goal line, willing to straight arm anyone in her way. Alvin was a small kid by any standard, but he was not embarrassed by her attention, he reveled in it.

Charlie was quiet, maybe even stoic if that's possible for someone that age. She would often wink at him and say, "I've got my eye on you Charlie Cossack, still waters run deep." He'd always smile back, but I'm not sure anyone of us understood what she meant.

As for me, a nick-name was born. During attendance, before desks were assigned, she peered about the classroom, looking for someone or something.

"Is the man with two first names here, Noah Gregory, are you gracing us today with your presence?"

Everyone laughed, and for me it was a great stress reliever, I kind of stood out in a good way, but the moniker stuck. Coaches, bosses, teachers, at one point or another, referred to me as the man with two first names. I didn't mind, I guess I've never found it derogatory, since it was originated by Sister Mary Bridget. It always makes me think of her and where she may be today. The buzz among the adults was she left the order to get married. I hope so, she always told great stories about her four brothers and the fun she had with them. God had no intention of denying her a family of her own.

"Gentlemen, the best way to overcome a fear is to face it." She was serious but not stern.

During the air raid drill, the three of us had exposed some vulnerabilities, I guess I should re-phrase that. We were piss your pants scared. Charlie vomited, Alvin held his ears and rolled on the floor, and I simply refused to come out from under my desk. When I lived with my real parents I was told to hide under the kitchen sink when they weren't home, and not to come out, or heaven forbid answer the door. If I did, someone would take me away from them. Looking back, that was the behavior I resorted to on the first air raid drill of the school year. There was something big going on that all the adults were talking about, I didn't understand it at the time, but the fear of a nuclear attack had become alarmingly real.

So, our assignment was to follow Mr. D and watch him crank the siren for the next drill. He met us at our classroom and we followed him down the hall. He had a nice presence, always calm, always smiling and kind. He had a thick head of curly hair, meticulously combed, along with bushy black eyebrows which kissed at the bridge of his nose. There was, however, one disconcerting aspect about him. He had a hand with only stubs for fingers. I tried not to look at them, but it was difficult not to. Poor guy, he cleaned up a lot of vomit and urine during his tenure at St. Anthony's, due mostly to some overbearing shrews parading as brides of Christ, convincing children they would be doomed to hell for harboring a bad thought but for a moment. Even Sister Mary Bridget acted differently when the old crows descended upon her classroom. It was noticeable, and when they darkened the doorway, the laughing stopped, the smiling stopped, only their cold stares persisted.

"Everything is going to be all right boys, cover your ears if you want to, but rest assured, nothing bad is going to happen. Any questions?"

"Did the Japs chop off your fingers?" Charlie Cossack asked the million dollar question everyone else was afraid to ask. He did it. One fear down for the day.

"Some very angry soldiers did some very bad things to me and my friends Charlie, but that's water under the bridge now."

"Did they use a sword?"

"It doesn't matter what they used, what's done is done."

"Did you shoot any of 'em?"

"I never shot anyone Charlie, I was lucky that way."

"I would've shot all of 'em."

"Let me tell you guys something, if you spend your lives trying to get even, you're never going to get ahead, you'll never amount to anything."

Tony rolled his shirt sleeve up to observe the second hand on his watch as he cranked the siren, leaving his maimed hand in full view of his entourage. A much scarier sight than the silly siren which now echoed through the hallways of St. Anthony's Academy.

I don't think Charlie accepted what he had been told, he was always fixated on revenge, but he backed off on the questioning and our assignment was a success. No pants pissing, puking, or passing out. Mission accomplished. Tony DiFabio marched his triumphant battalion back to the classroom single file, three proud soldiers who had spit in the face of death.

YOU MADE A GIRL CRY

OCTOBER
1969

There were some things that just weren't done, but these prohibitions always came with exclusions. During a schoolyard fight, no one was to be kicked in the balls, there was to be no choking or biting, and if someone was pinned to the ground by virtue of his arms, the oppressor didn't have the right to keep punching away at the fallen combatant's face. If someone gave in, that was to be the end of the conflict, simple enough. But there was something else, though never verbalized, which was understood as an unspoken rule. Men and boys should never make a girl cry. There are few things more demoralizing than seeing a girl or woman cry. Many of us had experienced this through our mothers, toughing out marriages with drunks, abusers, and cheaters.

"You broke my heart," a woman holding a hand to her chest, weeping, the mascara running down her cheeks. Once you experience the nausea that scene creates, you'll never wish to repeat it. There's something so disturbing about disappointing your mother, wife, or girlfriend, and the grief it induces, it haunts your soul.

But there is always someone willing to push the envelope, someone above all the rules, spoken or unspoken, someone by virtue of size or malice, who thinks the rules don't apply to him. That is why exceptions to rules exist. There is really only one exception. If someone bigger and meaner pushes the envelope, there is no dishonor in exacting retribution by any means possible. Biting, kicking, choking, double teaming, triple teaming, have at it boys – just be sure to leave a missing tooth or two. Leave a reminder for everyone to see. Break the rules and you will be punished. That's the lesson. Never forget a right, never forgive a wrong, from playground to adulthood, that was the credo we swore to live by.

Lili-Che Faithful sat in front of me in Religious Education class. I spent most of my time trying to make her laugh. Each giggle a victory. She was the most beautiful girl I had ever seen. A dark complexion and jet black hair, her speaking punctuated with a Hispanic accent, and the cologne she wore was hypnotic. And when she said my name – I was gob-smacked, speechless, a silly smile glued to my face.

She had her fair share of adversity as most eighth graders who don't exactly fit in do. She wasn't white, and she was pretty, so the other girls had her in their sights. Once in a while I'd hear a racial slur thrown her way. I'm sure she heard it too, but she never reacted. We had a student in a wheel chair for a short while, and Lili was assigned to wheel her from class to class. There weren't any elevators, so the custodian would carry her up and down, while Lili handled the in-betweens, including the rest room. She didn't seem to mind, she always had a smile on her face, and the two of them were often sharing laughs between classes. I overheard Lili teaching the girl some phrases in Spanish, and when that sweet language rolled off Lili's tongue, I became paralyzed, held hostage by the fantasies bouncing about my head.

The handicapped girl moved to a more accessible school after a few months, but Lili's war of kindness never ceased. She and her brother had been adopted by a missionary couple who moved back to the area from somewhere in Central America, so I've always believed their influence may have been behind her ruthless acts of generosity. But nonetheless, Lili was just one of those people who always did the right thing, said the right thing, and thought the right thing at the absolute worst of times. I admired and envied her for that. That wasn't me, never would be.

One chilly spring morning, Alvin Bean showed up in the park across from St. Anthony's Academy dressed only in a pair of Boy Scout pants. No shirt, no shoes, no socks, just a blank stare on his face. Students gathered in the park before morning bell, grouped in cliques, sneaking cigarettes and spreading gossip among their peers. Alvin stood alone. Soon, a group of older kids began taunting him and throwing chestnuts his way. I felt bad for him, but I did nothing to intercede. Lili, however, emerged from the school with the custodian, Mr. DiFabio. Lili wrapped a blanket around Alvin, and Mr. Difabio carried him to the nurse's office. I made eye contact with Lili during this episode, and I could sense her disappointment in me. We didn't see Alvin for a few months, but after the incident in the park, I swore never to disappoint Lili again.

During this time, my buddy Dagger and I had been receiving some harsh treatment from an older bully. He liked to cuff us in the back of our heads with an outstretched hand when we lined up for the bus in the morning. Typical prick. Big for his age and not all that smart. But the straw that broke the camel's back came when he pushed Lili out of the way when she was using the pencil sharpener one day during study hall.

"Gonna cry darkie? Get over it."

I was about to confront him then and there when Dagger grabbed me by the shirt and hauled me back.

"He'll kick your ass in front of the whole school, now's not the time."

Dagger was a thinker, and he could be a cruel son-of-a-bitch. He got the name Dagger after he attacked his sister's boyfriend with a steak knife. She was older, kind of wild, and the boyfriend was smacking her around in front of their house. Alan, his real name, took a few punches to the face, but he managed to inflict a couple stab wounds in the process. He was charged with assault, but the charges were reduced and he spent a year on probation along with weekly trips the County Mental Health Clinic.

"Do the math Charlie, we double team that asshole, we get him on the ground, we don't let him up, our only advantage is to keep him on the ground – I mean it, we have to mess him up hard, if he gets up we've had it."

And that we did. The next morning at the bus stop Mickey Hillman made the mistake of his life when he cuffed Dagger in the back of the head. Dagger responded with a quick shove back.

Infuriated, Mickey had Dagger by the throat with a finger pointed in his face. Dagger bit the finger with all his might, not letting go through the flurry of punches he was receiving. My cue had come. Enter Charlie Cossack, a berserker, a flat out homicidal maniac with nothing but revenge in his heart.

I grabbed Mickey by his tie and yanked while at the same time delivering a swift kick to his balls. He folded and fell to the ground, minus the tip of his finger which Dagger spit out, blood trickled from the corners of his mouth.

And then the ugly got even uglier. We kicked, we punched, we kicked and punched some more. I had him pinned to the ground, delivering blow after blow to his face, breaking my hand in the process. Two wolves had entered the pasture and descended upon their prey, two feral animals, survival of the fittest. Mickey, you're not getting up today, I'll have my revenge, you'll wear your nose ear to ear, and if you ever come near Lili again I'll rip your fucking head off.

We could hear the bus in the distance. Mickey was motionless, sobbing, bleeding profusely from his nose and mouth. The other students stood in awe. It had been so vicious, so primal, there were no chants for more, no crowding around, no one wanted to witness any more of this carnage. Dagger and I stood panting, but victorious, without a shred of regret or sympathy. What goes around comes around. You can take that to the bank. From now on there will be power in numbers. You may win today, but it will be a hollow victory, we will always demand retribution, and retribution will be ours. I had released something within me I was unable to control, and I could not have cared less. This wanton act of cruelty left me fulfilled, fuck the consequences.

From out of the crowd, Diane Lemon approached the wounded animal. Mickey would start his mornings at the bus stop by insulting Diane. Her braces, her acne, her glasses, anything and everything a teenage girl didn't want to hear, and her sisters would do nothing to intercede. They were embarrassed by her, they wouldn't defend her, so today, Diane stood alongside Mickey and kicked him in the small of his back while at the same time returning the stares of her two sisters.

"Call me pimple-puss now, you dirty bastard."

Dagger and I walked to school, avoiding the bus just pulling into the parking lot. The bus driver phoned the police and ambulance from a nearby house, but we were already gone. We were arrested that morning at school, led out by two cops and Sister Rene. The student body peered from windows and doorways, but I didn't look back. I could only imagine the disappointment on Lili-Che's face. I knew she wouldn't condone what I had done on any level, and if she witnessed the attack, she would have been brought to tears. So much for unspoken rules I thought, so much for honor, so much for making things right. I had done the impossible, abject failure achieved through victory.

As the patrol car pulled away with the two of us seated in the back, Dagger caught my eye, a half smile upon his face.

"Good thing he wasn't wearing a clip-on, huh?"

THE VEGETABLE GARDEN

UPSTATE SKILLED NURSING
UTICA, NY
1987

Ambulance crews transported patients back and forth from the hospital to the nursing home on a regular basis. Feeding tubes and artificial airways needed to be inspected monthly. The ambulance personnel often referred to the ward in which Tony DiFabio was head of housekeeping as "The Vegetable Garden," or "Site of the Living Dead."

Tony overheard these comments on numerous occasions. He didn't like them, but he didn't challenge them either. Sometimes, in the worst of situations, a morbid sense of humor makes life just a little bit more tolerable, and it was hard to overstate the obvious in regards to the patients residing in this ward.

Comatose, catatonic, completely oblivious to any stimulation from the outside world, these patients existed solely in a universe of their own. Tony often wondered if they could somehow communicate with each other in a language composed of thoughts, not words.

Tony moved his mop from side to side in a smooth uninterrupted fashion, taking pride in every stroke, the odor of disinfecting fluid wafting around him, enhanced by the floor fan positioned just inside the door.

Tony always spoke to the patients, wishing them a good day and a comfortable rest. He was finishing his floor mopping in a private room now, a room which housed a patient Tony remembered from years ago, from the years Tony spent as a custodian at St. Anthony's Academy. A student who stood out for his oddities and suffered for it. Although he knew him, the patient was unrecognizable, struck by a vehicle, the patient's head had swollen to twice the size of normal, and his eyes continually blinked, as is if he was ready to open them, but he never did.

"I know you're in there Alvin – it's me again, Tony D. Everything is going to be okay, just keep resting, we'll take good care of you."

Tony checked his watch. Quitting time. The floor was dry enough now to disconnect the fan and remove the caution sign from the hallway. Tony pushed the mop bucket into the hallway and turned to inspect his work before calling it quits for the day.

"Good night Alvin, see you tomorrow."

Alvin Bean tried his best to respond, hearing every word Tony had uttered, but to no avail once again. It would be a couple hours before Mrs. Makovitch would arrive to read to him. Most often the daily paper followed by an article from Popular Mechanics or National Geographic. How nice it would be to hear her gentle, soothing voice, just like first grade all over again, only this time, Mrs. Makovitch was the teacher, and the only thing missing would be a song on the piano before milk break. All the elementary teachers could play piano then, and it was great fun around Christmas time when the day ended with a few carols. Alvin tried to hum "Jingle Bells," but his vocal cords remained paralyzed.

But now it was time to get back to work. Since the accident, the coma had brought Alvin a sense of peace he never knew, and within this peace, Alvin was busy creating a perfect world. He no longer suffered from the inability to hold a thought in his head, or to sort through the overwhelming number of thoughts in his head. His thinking had become laser focused, crystal clear. The fear was gone, the elation was gone, the crippling depression had faded away. All that remained was a sense of calm balanced by the knowledge he was exactly where he needed to be. A serene limbo where anything was possible.

Just yesterday he devised and built a solar powered machine which cheaply and efficiently desalinates ocean water. No more droughts. Clean water for the entire planet. And in order to move this water he built an underground web of pipelines traversing through continents and over any mountains in the way. The Grand Canyon was now a rain forest, along with the Sahara Desert. Plants and trees are eating carbon dioxide and spitting out oxygen as it was meant to be. Greenhouse gases are perfectly balanced in the atmosphere. Solar and hydroelectric energy power the entire planet. The Great Lakes have been purified and re-circulate themselves through a series of solar powered pumps, which in turn spin turbines creating electricity.

Tiny batteries power vehicles in this world, and they are charged by inconspicuous solar panels woven into highways and the bodies of the automobiles themselves. Humans are no longer carnivores. Plants, vegetables, and fruits have been engineered to taste like meat and seafood, along with providing any needed protein. This Thanksgiving, families will grow turkeys in their gardens, no need to slaughter a bird, or any other creature again. Animal populations are monitored and simply controlled by birth control and natural selection.

There are, however, problems to be solved. The remaining nuclear waste needs to be disposed of along with anything that's not bio-degradable. Maybe a fleet of rockets launched into the sun or a technique to speed up radioactive half-life. And the speed of light and the whole perpetual motion thing, and controlling weather, there's a lot to solve. And if Alvin can figure out how to extend a human life into eternity, he'll need a sure fire way to get people off world and onto habitable planets, or at the very least into hollowed out asteroids. So much to do, but first Alvin has been thinking of presenting Mrs. Makovitch with a gift today, a simple display of gratitude. She deserves one. It wasn't her fault she ran over Alvin with her car, she needs to accept that and move on. She's lived too long to feel such remorse for something she was not responsible for.

As of late, Alvin has felt a strong connection between himself and the noises he hears from beyond his window. In the morning, when the nurse arrives to check his vitals, she opens the drapes and comments to him on the view of the courtyard.

"It's a sunny day Alvin, and Tony is filling the feeders, still no orioles as far as I can see."

Tony has been obsessed with luring orioles to his feeders. In addition to the seed, he leaves out slices of oranges and Mason jar lids filled with jam, but no luck so far. Tony is a patient man, and he won't give up. They'll show sooner or later, he's sure of that.

In the meantime, Alvin has been focusing on the chirping coming from the feeders, hoping on some level to speed the arrival of the orioles. He doesn't feel them, but yesterday he felt the arrival of something else, something many of us will never experience, and probably don't even know exists.

Today, Mrs. Makovitch will have her reading interrupted by a tapping on the window. When she opens the drapes to see what is making that noise, she will be greeted by an unexpected visitor peeking back at her. A visitor invited to this window courtesy of Alvin Bean. A cardinal, but no ordinary cardinal, a pure white cardinal, a spectacular white, bathed in the light of the setting afternoon sun.

Although the encounter will only last for a second or two, Mrs. Makovitch will pivot from the window just as fast, hoping to share news of this encounter with someone, anyone. Mrs. Makovitch will drop the newspaper she carried with her to the window as she realizes another unexpected gift.

"Alvin, you're smiling."

AN ARMY OF SECOND BASEMEN

THE ELMIRA PIONEERS
JULY 1975

The coach sat down next to me on the bench and forcefully put his hand on my shoulder. He was chubby and balding, and was never without a chaw of tobacco in his mouth. The black tar most often dripped down his chin. He would calmly wipe it away with his sleeve.

"Noah," he began, "you know what happens when you shake a tree?"

I'd heard this before and I knew why he was saying this to me. I didn't reply, I knew what was coming.

"Well, a second baseman falls out."

Then he tried to soften the blow but failed miserably.

"You've got speed, you're an excellent fielder and you do all right at bat, but you're not a standout, and that's what it takes to move on as a second baseman."

In his own way, this fat bastard wannabe was trying to save me from the fate that befell him. I know, I know – go to college, learn a trade, become a cop or a firefighter, coach kids in your hometown and lament to them on how close you came to almost making it. Well, you know what, that's just not good enough for me. It never will be.

I swallowed hard and resisted the urge to punch him in that giant vanilla moon pie he called a face. He waddled towards the field, his cleats scraping against the dugout floor. So much for fatherly advice I thought. But guys like me don't take fatherly advice. Guys like me always bring their suitcases to the ballpark. Guys like me always carry just enough cash to get home.

This time felt different though, painfully different. Some of this I would never miss – the bus rides, the junk food, the flea bag motels, and the broken dreams, especially the broken dreams. One stinging disappointment after another, a never ending cavalcade of failure. I'd heard it all before.

"You got guts kid, but you're no Rod Carew, you're just nothing special."

Fuck all of you. The scouts, the coaches, the shitty hometown newspapers. You've left me no choice, I'll have my revenge. I'll assemble a ruthless horde of second basemen. A rag tag army of guys with colossal hearts and even bigger balls. Guys who play hurt. Guys who play with taped ankles and knees, guys who would rather commit suicide than let a sore toe keep them out of the lineup.

When we're slumping at the plate, we bunt, we've mastered the art of stepping into a pitch to reach first base, and when we get there it's a sure bet we'll steal second. And it's not just any stolen base, we come in hard, we come in spikes up, and we don't give a flying fuck if someone does that to us the next inning. And when we're hot at the plate, it's because we're hitting to the opposite field, we're hitting to where you aren't. Simple as that. So tell your catchers to take heed, because when we're headed home nothing stops us. Block the plate at your own peril and eat my shoulder. Safe or out, I'll trot to the dugout afterwards as coaches and umpires gather around you. Their concern means nothing to me because you were warned and you chose to ignore it.

We don't commit errors in the infield, and our outfielders execute elaborate relay throws to tag runners out. It is precision and elegance, all in one. It is math and science mixed with pure determination. It is everything you are not. Try us motherfucker, we'll gun you out at home. Our pitchers throw an eclectic blend of garbage. Knuckleballs, roundhouse curves, and sliders are on the menu, and just when you get comfortable, they'll sneak one by you at the letters. Strike three. Have a seat asshole.

I'll take my army barnstorming. We'll play anyone who dares. Fill Yankee Stadium and bring Ruth and Gehrig back from the dead, Mantle and Maris in their prime, I don't give a shit. But you won't do that because you know what I know – we won't give up, we'll make your best not good enough.

Yes, the world needs an army of second basemen. My army.

THE BEE KEEPER

NEVADA / CALIFORNIA BORDER
1988

I recently purchased a beautiful home in a remote mountain town straddling the Nevada/California border. It allows me to make frequent trips to Reno on behalf of my employer, and to visit Yosemite, which has become a respite for me. It's a quaint little house in a quaint little city full of quaint little houses like mine.

We experience the four seasons here, an abbreviated version, but the four seasons nonthetheless, so in terms of post card appeal, we have it all. When I stroll through town on sunny afternoons, I am expecting to see Norman Rockwell seated at an easel in his front yard, a pipe clenched between his teeth.

Although picture perfect, we do get an occasional transient or two, usually a broken down van or camper with the occupants unable to afford the needed repairs to keep moving. After a few days the Sheriff has the vehicle towed, the repairs made, and urges the visitors to never return.

A few months ago an unusual guest arrived via bicycle, the kind of bike you might see in the yellowed pages of an old Sears Christmas Catalogue. That book of dreams we worshipped as children. Obviously an antique, the bike appeared to be in excellent condition. It was pedaled furiously by an individual wearing a bee keeper's helmet, complete with a shroud and netting.

This individual appeared so strange to me that I knew it was inevitable we would meet. Someone of that ilk is drawn to me by a force greater than magnetism or gravity. I'm not sure why, I never have been, but it's been a constant in my life since childhood. I was once told that the longer one avoids his fate, the sooner he will meet it. Maybe I should just get it over with. He probably needs a few bucks, maybe something to eat, maybe a bus ticket if he's rational enough to have a destination.

Nah, I thought, there's no chance I'll be able to defy my life-long pattern, when we meet, it'll be on his terms. Besides, I was disturbed enough by witnessing someone in that condition, I didn't need to find out why. It's always so much more uncomfortable to find out how and why someone finds themselves lost in their own mind and the circumstances surrounding it. Nah, I was three months without a drink or a line of cocaine, I didn't need a sob story or the ravings of a pathetic wretch to trigger something within me. It never took much for me to fall off the wagon, and when I fall, I fall hard.

I bumped into the Sheriff a few mornings after our guest arrived. We frequented the same diner for breakfast and occasionally engaged in small talk. Our stranger had set up camp on the edge of town and the Sheriff was on his way to encourage an immediate departure. The Sheriff finished his coffee and left, but not without reminding me to say hello to my employer for him. In reality we both worked for the same guy, the Sheriff, however, was a few rungs below me.

A couple minutes later I finished eating and cashed out, late again as usual. I wasn't looking forward to the three hour drive to Reno or the ass chewing I would be subjected to by my employer's associates. They were always in a hurry, always in miserable moods, always warning me what would happen if I messed up with the suitcase full of counterfeit money they were handing me.

Upon exiting the diner, the "bee keeper" rushed towards me with his right arm extended, a small white box in his hand, a box similar to what a piece of jewelry would be packaged in, perhaps a bracelet. His silent offering left me more curious than surprised. As I opened the box, the stranger pedaled away. Inside the box was a key, we used to call them skeleton keys, and it was probably much older than the bicycle I could see fading in the distance.

There is a shell of a brick house thousands of miles away from this sleepy mountain town, a large house, a cold house, the house where I lived as a child. There was a closet in this house that locked with a key such as I was now holding. Nothing good ever came from that closet, no one was allowed to enter that closet, and that closet remained locked until as a child I found the key, maybe the key I now had in my hand. I'd heard noises coming from that closet deep into sleepless nights, but I was always told it was just a dream, or I was imagining it.

"Hannigan," my mother would say, "you have such an imagination, we don't go in that closet because the floor is crumbling, and besides, we don't have a key."

One day I dropped a quarter and it rolled under my dresser. I needed that quarter and I was in a hurry. I didn't like being upstairs in that house alone. It always felt as if someone was standing next to me when they weren't. I quickly got down on all fours and felt around under the dresser. Yes, I could feel the quarter surrounded by clumps of dust, but when I pulled it out a skeleton key came with it.

I pocketed them both. I wanted to leave, to run downstairs and out into the sunshine, but I knew it was time to get it over with, to face my fear, to put an end to the demons haunting my imagination. I walked defiantly to that closet and inserted the key. I heard the click of the mechanism as the door creaked open.

I awoke in the hospital, my mother beside the bed. She told me it was a seizure, but I knew it was not. Something else had robbed me of my memory, something dark and cruel. Later that week our house burned down, and the Fire Chief kept asking me why I set the fire, but I kept saying I didn't do it. He didn't believe me, but my mother did. Or at least she said she did.

A GRAND UNIFIED DILEMMA

THE WHITE CARDINAL RANCH
PATAGONIA, SOUTH AMERICA
2072

Since its release in 2052, the Humanity Virus had blanketed the Earth. The original infection, confined to migratory birds, transmitted rapidly to domesticated birds before beginning a random game of tag, hopping to and fro, from species to species, finally burrowing into the human population.

Originally engineered to combat cancer by virtue of antibody creation, the virus had some amazing side effects. Once infected, and after the incubation period, not only did cancer cells disappear, but neurons in the human brain fired at a spectacular rate, the human mind evolved centuries into the future, and with that, mental illness and emotional irrationality had been confined to history. They no longer posed a threat to society. Hate and division evaporated, rage and envy no longer infected the minds of the privileged or the downtrodden. The human race ushered in an age of peace and enlightenment. And, most significantly, these antibodies were passed genetically from parent to child.

Soldiers laid down their arms and walked off the battlefield, borders and disagreements surrounding them now meant nothing. Governments existed only to benefit humanity as a whole, problems such as poverty and hunger were eradicated within a decade. The most important aspect of a human's life was now Happiness, not riches or power. It became a healthy competition to see who, whether an individual or group, could do more to benefit humanity, but now, twenty years later, a dilemma was identified.

Sofia Faithful had summoned the creators of the Humanity Virus to her compound at the White Cardinal Ranch. This group was composed of researchers from every branch of science and mathematics, and clergy from every known faith, to whom she would today present with a dilemma, a looming crisis that if not resolved, would lead to catastrophic suffering.

The average lifespan of a human was now projected to be nearly 120 years. Sofia herself was 90 years old and had just completed a daily five mile run due to the avalanche of advancements in medical technology and health care. There were no wars, the few remaining diseases were rare and curable, and most amazingly, there had not been a suicide reported since 2059.

One school of thought projected the possibility of an eternal human life span within the next half century, and that was the dilemma. Humans would simply run out of room on planet Earth, becoming nothing more than a pile of ants on the remains of a sugar cube.

The newly evolved human brain could not fathom an end to procreation, that in itself had become the largest Happiness motivator, superior to laughter and the arts. Happiness had now become equally as important as oxygen to human survival.

It would take at least another 200 years to fully terra-form Mars into a habitable planet, and the colonies on the moon were still at odds with long term radiation exposure. Earth just didn't have the time to wait. Sofia stood at the podium, four composition notebooks laid on the table next to her, the four composition notebooks that enabled the creation of the Humanity Virus. The notebooks were discovered in her late step-father's belongings and brought to her attention by her mother. Each composition notebook, numbered 1 thru 4, was labeled with A.B. on its cover. No other identifiers of the author existed.

"I have presented you with the dilemma, the end of humanity as we now know it within fifty years, but I can now propose solutions, solutions that may carry severe consequences."

Members had been summoned to the auditorium instead of appearing by hologram due to the importance of this announcement. The human psyche now rejoiced in solving problems, the harder the better, solve the unsolvable, but this problem had no comfortable solutions.

"My team has decoded the remaining equations in the notebooks, we thought the math just wasn't there, but all along it was, it just wasn't the type of math we understood, but now we have in a sense, discovered a whole new understanding of mathematics, or what A.B. perceived mathematics to be."

Dr. Claude Higbee walked slowly to the podium while Sofia seated herself. Dr. Higbee, a renowned astrophysicist, looked down upon the composition notebooks with reverence as he began his presentation. It was his strong conviction and twenty years of work that led to the translation of A.B.'s equations listed in the fourth of the notebooks.

"I can state today, with 100 percent scientific certainty, that the translated equations have elegantly, and succinctly, led to the Grand Unified Theory we have searched for since Einstein introduced us to Relativity and the problems it encountered with Quantum Mechanics. Dark Matter, String Theory, and the expansion of the universe are now completely understandable along with a new definition of gravity. Notebook #4 can be used as a road map to lead us off planet. We now have the ability to move millions of light years in hours not eons, but I must present you with a worst case scenario. There is a possibility that by opening gateways to other galaxies, we may accidentally rip a hole in space and time, we may, and I repeat this is not a certainty, create a chain reaction which could reverse the space and time continuum in seconds. But I need to also remind you this is not the first time man has wrestled with this. Before splitting the atom these fears were also realized."

Sofia returned to the podium. Dr. Higbee stood at her side.

"I would like to personally thank Claude for the decades of work he put into translating the equations in Notebook #4 and for presenting us with a viable option for saving Happiness as we now understand it. But I need to add that getting to habitable worlds is only the beginning of the solution. There is a greater than average chance those planets are already inhabited with life which has existed for millions, maybe billions of years. We don't know that yet, it may take decades of exploration to find worlds which could give us what we now enjoy here, perhaps centuries of loneliness and strife, and in the process we are risking an end to the universe. It is only fair to present you with another option."

Dr. Higbee appeared uneasy, he looked downwards, his face drawn. Obviously, he was willing to take the chance on getting off planet, feeling the risks paled in comparison to the benefits. But, Sofia's counterpoints were valid, and since her discovery of the notebooks as a child, she had changed the world into something philosophers could only opine on. It was her creativity and drive which had turned Earth into a paradise, the Garden of Eden once again. He raised his head and poised himself to hear her answer to the problem, a problem he had helped create.

"This solution will make you very uncomfortable, it sickens me to even mention it, but I must. We have the ability to re-engineer the Humanity Virus, to make it undo all the good it has done. By doing so, populations will again endure the effects of violence, pestilence, avarice, and sorrow. The evil and the greedy will gain footholds once again, and through all this, the human population will be controlled, there will be no need to move off planet. Happiness will no longer be innate, it will be the responsibility of the individual to find a path to it once again. The individual will need to foster benevolence and altruism without the assistance of a virus. Maybe this is how it was meant to be, maybe we should just acknowledge that without this struggle we are less than human."

Sofia held up Notebook #1 and leafed to the last page, displaying it to the audience. On that page, A.B. had drawn a road sign, colored yellow and shaped as a diamond, with black capital letters spelling out: HOPE.

DO FLEAS HAVE FLEAS

ST. ANTHONY'S ACADEMY
1973

Noah Gregory sat motionless, his head upon the table, supported by his forearms. Detention once again and he was joined by the usual cast of characters in the Library. Diane sat across from him, eager to talk, to ramble on and to hang on his every word. It was no secret she had a crush on him. Noah was always polite to her, never condescending, or pitiful of her. She had a tough go of it he thought. Her two sisters were popular and pretty. Diane was neither. Her sisters were as cruel to her as the rest of the school. Poor girl, she spent a lot of time in remedial classes, and she misbehaved only to serve detention along with Noah. She spoke rapid fire, interweaving laughter with language that at times bordered upon incoherence. Her glasses were habitually smudged and her braces often had the trace of lunch or breakfast upon them.

At an adjacent table sat Kelly and Kennedy. Two glue sniffing sadists who delighted in tossing spit wads at Diane when the librarian wasn't looking. It happened so frequently Diane didn't react anymore. Noah despised those two. Anything for a laugh at someone else's expense. Rumor had it they were beating up bums at the depot and snatching purses from old ladies after Bingo. Pukes, Noah thought, nothing but pukes.

After arriving late to school one day, subsequent to his favorite breakfast of marijuana and screwdriver, Noah noticed Diane's hair had been peppered with spit wads, and he knew who the culprits were. Something about doing booze with marijuana always left Noah a little angry when he was coming down as he so often did in detention. That day he abruptly went to a book shelf and grabbed a large volume of an encyclopedia and proceeded towards his assigned table, but on the way he gave the book a good old fashioned baseball swing, twice. One for each of the glue sniffers. The thumps were solid, they resonated like good wood on a homerun. They both fell out of their chairs. Noah casually sat down and began thumbing through the pages. The librarian never looked up and the glue sniffers did nothing but rub their heads and re-seat themselves. Smart move on their part. Noah would have liked nothing better than to mix it up that day. Nothing but pukes he thought. A smile stretched across Diane's face, but she knew not to engage Noah in conversation, nothing needed to be said.

But today, Noah had a new sense of uneasiness. Some paranoia was beginning to set in. He had spent most of the last week smoking pot, a substantial increase in his usual consumption. Two or three times a day along with a pint or two of screwdriver. He didn't like feeling like this, he didn't like experiencing the fear and uncomfortable inertia that accompanied it. He decided to put his head down until the uneasiness abated. Maybe a short nap would do the trick.

He awoke to Diane gently shaking his arm. He looked about and realized what she was alerting him to.

"He's back," she whispered.

"Yes he is."

Noah sighed and shifted his chair back. His fingers laced behind his head. Yes, Alvin Bean is in the library, and he is wearing his Civil Air Patrol uniform, and when he wears his Civil Air Patrol uniform he is most often off his medications, and when he is off his medications he is at his most talkative, and when he is talkative, there is no better victim than Noah.

"Hi Noah, I've got something to tell you."

"I bet you do."

Alvin seated himself next to Diane and quietly laid a text book on the table. His complexion was greasy and dotted with blackheads, there were scabs on his temples, the result of some earlier acne removal, and he sported a brush cut, a fashion disaster for any high school student in the year 1973. He focused his glassy eyes squarely upon Noah, as if taking aim.

Diane was eagerly anticipating the conversation. Her eyes darted between Noah and Alvin. The glue sniffers were busy attempting some do it yourself tattoos with a razor blade and a ball point pen, oblivious to Alvin's entrance.

"I talked to Professor Otto on my ham radio last night, he's onto something big."

Alvin would often fixate on Professor Otto, a mystery man who contacted him via short wave radio. The radio bit was likely true, the roof of Alvin's house was littered with antennas and Alvin was quite good with electronics, but the Professor Otto thing had to be bullshit. A charter member of St. Anthony's AV Club, Alvin most likely inherited his father's penchant for that sort of thing. His father worked for a local TV cable company and ran the Civil Air Patrol branch in the city.

"Doctor Otto is investing in miniature robots, it's fascinating."

"I give, what's so fascinating about tiny robots?"

"Think about it, they can be put into our bodies to cure diseases – to kill cancer cells and ream out plugged arteries."

"Wouldn't they have to be very, very small, what the fuck Alvin, how can someone build a robot that small, it's flat out impossible."

"Otto has built a whole civilization of tiny robots that have built even smaller robots, and so on and so forth. They're so freakin' small now you can't even see them with a microscope. No shit."

Hold on a second, Noah thought about it, maybe it was just the pot or the booze, but Alvin might be on to something here. Makes a lot more sense than his plan for Smell-O-Vision, which Noah always thought had been plagiarized from a comic book or some other off beat source.

"How about I come over to your house tonight and talk to Professor Otto about this myself."

"You won't be able to. Dr. Otto is maintaining radio silence for the next week. Spies are trying to steal his inventions, and he has to be very careful."

Noah had to give Alvin credit, he always had an answer, and it was always delivered without hesitation.

Diane adjusted her glasses and decided to weigh in on the topic.

"After all Noah, how do we know that fleas don't have fleas?"

Now that's an uncomfortable thought. Noah sensed a new wave of paranoia taking hold, and gently laid his head back down on the table. His forearms crossed.

"You've hit the nail on the head Diane," Alvin's voice deepened, bolstered by Diane's apparent vindication of him.

"Fleas absolutely do have fleas!"

A ROAD MAP AND SOME NO-DOZE

SOMEHWERE IN RURAL PENNSYLVANIA
1988

Naomi Clearwater is traveling through the late hours of a humid summer night, a full moon her only companion. She's fresh out of a truck stop restroom, the worst kind, the filthiest kind. She pops her last two No-Doz and hits the road again. As the miles drag on, dew begins to form on the windshield, the wipers groan as she turns them on then off, on then off. She's been driving for hours, making her way to a family emergency three states away. Her brother is in desperate need of a transplant, there's a donor organ, but the whole situation is touch and go according to her mother.

The only radio station she can receive is replaying news from the day before. She's listened to it so long she can repeat the stories verbatim. She unwraps a stick of chewing gum and slowly pushes it into her mouth. Anything to stay awake, but the pills help the most. She'll need more of them.

An hour passes and then another, and then another. She catches sight of herself in the rear view mirror, her pupils look strange, so much larger than usual. She decides it's time for a rest and a cup of coffee. She'll stop at the next all night diner and make a quick call on the pay phone there. Great, there's one coming up and there's a gas station next door.

"Two birds with one stone, yeah, two birds with one stone," she whispers.

As she fills up, a gaunt young man approaches.

"Hey lady, your back tire looks low."

He directs her to the rear of the car to have a look.

"I guess so," she replies, not really sure what she's looking at.

"Pull over to the air compressor and I'll fill it up for you."

He seems sincere, but his appearance has her ill at ease. His white t-shirt is torn and dirty. The ball cap he's wearing is ringed with salt stains from perspiration, and his hands are grease laden. Above his wrists are some amateurish attempts at tattoos, some misspelled. The compressor is under a light, and the store clerk is visible from inside the gas station. If he tries anything she can be into the store in seconds. After all, what could be worse than having a flat tire here. Here in the middle of nowhere.

She pulls to the compressor and he's already at the tire. No reason to step out. She can hear the dinging with each pulse of air pumped into the tire. She puts her window down to thank him. No reason to take a chance now.

"Better safe than sorry, yeah, better safe than sorry," she whispers.

He's visible in the side view mirror. He steps back, proud of his work. He approaches her open window.

"There you go, all set, but you better keep an eye on it."

He turns and walks hurriedly to his pick-up, still parked at the gas pumps. She waves in appreciation as he drives by, the muffler coughing black smoke into the night air.

She enters the diner, her car parked within a quick step of the front door. No sense in traversing parking lots alone at this time of night. She finds the phone and makes her call. Things sound better on the other end. Her mother may be downplaying the situation. She's good at that, but her demeanor relaxes Naomi. The only seating available until breakfast is at the counter. She looks for an empty seat, one with empty seating on either side. She finds it and orders coffee.

A man enters and sits next to her. He's different than the rest of the insomniacs and truck drivers seated around her. He's a massive man, but well dressed for his stature. A three piece suit, minus the tie, a gold chain showing from around his neck. His beard neat and close cropped, and his hair combed as if he'd just hopped out of a barber's chair. He orders his coffee and an order to go with a thick, interesting accent, but his English is flawless. She notices his hands, they're huge, his nails manicured. He could snap a neck as if it were a pencil.

He wants to talk. Naomi tries to ignore him at first, but there is something about his accent that lures her into a conversation.

"Where are you off to this time of night," he begins. Each word pronounced in flawless English, but the accent is unmistakable.

"Pittsburgh, my brother is having emergency surgery."

"Well, be careful, it's starting to fog up out there." He stirs cream into his coffee and continues.

"We're headed to Buffalo from Yonkers, but the driver got lost a few hours ago."

"You've got a while then, sounds like you need a new driver."

"He's one of those guys who can do anything, but nothing very well. The boss isn't happy, he's got some important business tomorrow."

"What do you guys do?"

"Stuff," the stranger chuckles and tucks a road map into the pocket of his suit coat. "Could've used this three hours ago."

"Stuff ?"

"I used to say I worked for the devil, but now the boss is more of an angel – he's had some sort of revelation, it feels like we've been on some sort of apology tour."

"Apology tour ?"

"Well, I used to think prison was going to be my retirement plan, but now it's looking more like I'll be hosting charity telethons – weird turn of events."

Naomi sips her coffee. She needs to get out of this conversation. Why is he telling her this, it's starting to feel uncomfortable. She needs an out. Then it comes. A waitress runs by her with a pitcher of water. She pours it into a smoldering waste basket which has just erupted into flames. Cigarette butts the cause. Naomi lays a couple of dollars onto the counter and makes her exit while her new friend watches the action. Customers applaud the waitress as Naomi is out the door and quickly into her car.

She turns the radio off and begins to analyze her conversation with the dapper giant. She checks the rear view mirror to make sure she's not being followed. Good, no headlights in sight. He must be spinning a tale to another unsuspecting listener. But, maybe, just maybe, he is who he said. Anything's possible. This thought intensifies because Naomi knows buried deep within each lie ever told is a kernel of truth, and the more outrageous the lie, the more we dig for that kernel of truth. It's just human nature. Naomi has lied plenty of times, most often with little consequence. Harmless white lies. Everyone has lied at one point or another, but some people are really good at it. They're the scary kind, the ones with the agendas.

So, what's his agenda, his motivation? Naomi reassures herself the stranger is merely a harmless embellisher, a bull-shitter with one weird pick-up line, someone dressing the part, and speaking the part, trying to be what he is not. Nevertheless, as a woman travelling alone, Naomi is vulnerable. That clerk eyeballing her three gas stations ago was intimidating, she should have told him to knock it off, but she didn't. It's easy to think that way now, but there's something about that guy in the diner Naomi just can't shake.

"Men, they're all liars, yeah, all liars," she whispers.

"Oh no, oh shit," she screams. The car wobbles as she finally manages to control the steering wheel. Must be that tire. "Fuck," she hollers as the car grinds to a halt, just off the roadway. There's nothing in sight before her, and it's at least a five mile walk back to the diner. She's never changed a tire, but maybe if she leaves the trunk up, someone will stop. She stares at the spare, but something's missing. It's just the tire, nothing else. She's not sure exactly what's missing, but she knows it's not good.

Wait, yes, she sees headlights approaching from the rear. She waves her arms up and down. The car is still running, the tail lights dimly illuminate her. A pick-up pulls behind her and the driver gets out. It's that skinny kid from the gas station. His headlights are blinding Naomi. He moves towards the trunk of her car and gazes in.

"You got no jack, can't change a tire without a jack."

He seems agitated, his voice grows louder with each word.

"Jump in the truck and I'll give you a ride to a tire shop."

"No thanks," Naomi murmurs, "I've got someone coming."

"You ain't got shit."

He grabs her by the wrist and begins pulling her towards his truck. He's stronger than his reed thin frame would lead you to believe. Naomi is paralyzed with fear. She's almost into the truck when headlights appear in the distance. As the vehicle nears, she fights with all her might, fear is feeding the adrenaline coursing through her body. She gets loose from his grasp just as the approaching vehicle stops adjacent to the truck.

It's a large vehicle, a limousine with tinted windows. A big man crawls out from the front passenger seat. It's the man from the diner. His head moves slowly from Naomi's car to the pick-up. Naomi is breathless and in tears. Another man exits from the driver's side and edges towards the skinny kid. The kid takes a step towards the open trunk of Naomi's car.

"Don't believe that bitch, she stole my wallet at the gas station back there, I followed her to get it back."

Her diner friend's associate takes a step closer to the kid. He's every bit as big as his partner. His clothing is disheveled. The suit collar is half-up, half-down, his dress shirt is un-tucked, and he sports thick glasses, glistening from the pick-up truck headlights. His moustache is un-kept and his English is broken. He struggles to form each word, obviously not his native tongue. Naomi follows his lips as he begins to speak.

"What you name kid?"

"What's it to ya, lard-ass," defiance now replacing anger in the assailant's voice.

The wrong answer delivered with a brazen attitude. In an instant the big man has the kid by the collar. He walks him to the back of the pick-up, the kid on his tip-toes.

"So you like hurt girls, eh?"

The big man lifts the kid by his belt and collar and knocks his head against the rear fender, multiple times, before depositing him into the bed of the truck.

"We can change your tire if you'd like." Naomi's diner friend speaks slowly and deliberately.

"I don't have a jack."

"No problem as long as you have a tire. Bohdan, leave the young gentleman and give me a hand, we're going to need a lug wrench as well."

Before approaching his partner, Bohdan kicks the headlights out of the assailant's truck. He retrieves something from the back of the limo and hands it to Naomi's friend. Naomi surmises the cross shaped tool must be a lug wrench.

Bohdan lifts the rear of Naomi's 1984 Plymouth Horizon as her friend hurriedly removes the tire and replaces it with the spare.

Naomi wonders what comes next. What is she in for now, and who in hell are these two giants. Her thoughts shift back to the pick-up as she hears a pathetic groan coming from the bed. It sounds like a muffled cry for help. Bohdan lumbers towards the truck as the rear window of the limo opens a crack and Naomi's diner friend takes something from the occupant.

"My employer would like you to have this in return for your discretion."

Before Naomi is presented with the thick, letter sized envelope, the stranger takes a pen from his suit coat pocket and scribbles something on it.

"There's enough in there for a new tire, maybe a new car, and if you'd like to have coffee again, my number is on the front. Just ask for the big guy, the good looking one."

Naomi jumps into the driver's seat of the Horizon and pokes her head out of the window.

"Shouldn't we call the cops on that kid ?"

"Nah, I'll have a chat with him."

"Hey Gennady," Bohdan shouts, "we gonna need shovel."

Naomi's friend smiles as her eyes grow wide. He winks and shoos her away with his massive hand.

She pulls her vehicle onto the roadway from the shoulder as a blazing morning sun rises behind her. She adjusts the rear view mirror to shield the glare from her eyes and looks down on her aching wrist. It's bruised and swollen. That kid must have messed with the tire, it's the only thing that makes sense, and that other guy must be who he says he is.

Naomi's instinct is to call the police, but why should she. She's probably not his first victim, but she'll be his last.

"Yeah, I'll be his last," she whispers.

ALVIN BEAN HAS LEFT THE BUILDING

UPSTATE SKILLED NURSING FACILITY
UTICA, NY
1987

Alvin Bean's mechanical life support systems had been disconnected. His only surviving relative, an aunt living in California, made the decision. Alvin's vitals were steadily growing worse and his brain activity was scientifically undetectable.

The nurse would hear the long, ear piercing tone when the time arrived. Tony DiFabio sat at the foot of Alvin's bed and said the Rosary. Tony had done this for the last three days since the decision was made. It had been a whirlwind of a month. Word spread about the comings and goings of a white cardinal at the facility's bird feeders and people were making constant requests to view the feeders from Alvin's room. It was not allowed, but one visitor did find his way in. Tony asked him to leave, but he became indignant and refused.

"Listen, I own this place, and I'm not hurting a thing, I'm the reason Alvin has this room, I'm the reason you have a job, get it?"

It was rumored Charlie Cossack had something to do with this facility. A local businessman, thought to be a racketeer and a drug dealer, now Tony had heard it from the horse's mouth.

Tony arose from his chair to stand forehead to forehead with the intruder.

"What happened to you Charlie, you were a good student, you had potential, now you burn buildings down and sell drugs."

"That's bullshit."

"You remember Billy Thomas, he's an Admiral, and John Cotton, he's a brain surgeon, and you – you wouldn't make a pimple on a real man's ass."

Infuriating. That phrase was infuriating. Charlie's father often used that phrase when angry with him, or more honestly, when angry with himself, looking to pin blame for his miserable existence on someone else, usually the nearest someone else. What the hell did it even mean?

"Here's the difference between you and me," Charlie cocked his head and clenched his fists.

"I'm not content to be a janitor, and if I were you, I'd still be hunting down those bastards who chopped my fingers off – you've eaten every plate of shit you've ever been served, and I'm never going to do that."

Charlie took a few short steps to the window. Tony sat down and returned to the Rosary, the hand crafted beads strung through the stubs on his right hand.

In the weeks after the cardinal arrived, rumors circulated about the good fortune people received by catching even a mere glimpse of the elusive bird. Diseases went into remission, the unemployed found work, and the most desperate and despondent among us became rejuvenated with a sense of hope and determination, all due to the brilliant white bird which visited the feeders and made momentary stops at Alvin Bean's window sill.

Charlie Cossack turned slowly and moved towards the door, trying to form an apology in his head. Mr. D was a good man, an American hero who didn't need to be lectured by the likes of a thug seeking redemption by throwing money around, doing favors, but always asking for something in return.

"I'm sorry Mr. D, I'm just sick of the stories about me floating around town. This place is spotless, I'll make sure you get a raise."

"I'll accept the apology, but the raise isn't necessary, I'm already making as much as the nurses and I've only been here a year, give them one."

"You deserve it, but I'll check into their salaries too. Guess the bird isn't showing today, huh?"

"It only shows for the right people Charlie."

"So, I'm not a good person then, what about Alvin, he never hurt anyone, why doesn't he just get out of bed now and get on his bicycle, there's no sense to this."

"It all makes perfect sense, you just don't understand it. The tragedy is you may never understand it."

Charlie Cossack sighed as he walked into the hallway. He had always liked Mr. DiFabio, everyone at St. Anthony's school did, but if Charlie stayed a second longer he would have unloaded on Tony again. After all Tony went through, the sacrifices he made for his country, and he settles for a job as a school janitor, simply crazy. Just another sanctimonious old man, secretly regretting the life he led, compensating for it with a sense of righteousness. Charlie had heard enough, better to just walk away.

Tony finished saying the Rosary and put the beads back into a small leather pouch, a gift presented to him over forty years ago by a Filipino priest. That was the day Japanese soldiers bayoneted the priest and amputated the fingers on Tony's right hand with one quick swing of an officer's sword. Tony put the pouch in his pocket and paused at the doorway for one last look at Alvin.

"It's okay to let go now Alvin, everything is going to be alright, I promise."

Deep within Alvin's mind a new adventure formed. Since the coma, Alvin had explored the universe with one significant exception. On his first journey, Alvin discovered a massive black hole which has been busy gobbling up the universe ever since the split second it had spit it out billions of years ago. Alvin was nearly pulled into the abyss on that journey, and he fled in fear. But now it was time to face that fear, it was time to put it to rest. Within this universe eating giant is a pin prick of light, and with every inch one nears this point of light, the brighter it becomes. Alvin decided it was time to find out what was on the other side. Another fear faced, another fear conquered.

HYPOTHERMIA

UTICA, NY
1965

The four of us watched the ambulance personnel remove the body from the house. We tried to get a peek, but the cadaver had been placed in a body bag before being placed on the stretcher. Mrs. Steinbrenner made the shocking discovery.

Claude, the cadaver, had moved into the neighborhood before any of us could remember. At our age then, everyone looked old to us, living or dead. Mrs. Steinbrenner was a widow and Claude was a widower, or so he said. Our parents thought it was wonderful the two of them had found each other. Summer afternoons on the porch, out to dinner on Fridays, and drives through the countryside on the weekends.

Mrs. Steinbrenner deserved that. Her husband had been an abusive alcoholic, but she never wavered from her roles as mother and grandmother. Her extended family shared the neighborhood praise for the relationship.

I heard my adoptive parents talking about Claude's death when they thought I was out of earshot. I was no stranger to suicide, my mother jumped off an overpass and my father hung himself by driving a framing nail through a belt and into the upper door casing separating the kitchen from the living room before looping the belt around his neck. I was three at the time, but I still have memories of trying to wake him as he swung back and forth from my nudging.

They were drug users and incapable of caring for themselves, let alone a child. I was once told that most coincidences take a lot of planning, but I'll share this one with you, as it was completely devoid of forethought. When my mom jumped off the over pass, my adoptive dad was driving down the road in a fire truck, a ladder truck to be precise. Her body fell directly in front of the truck. Imagine that, a body falling from the sky and landing feet from where your vehicle has been forced to stop. Astonished, but being the men they were, my dad and his crew did the best they could to revive her, but the extent of her injuries made their efforts futile.

Whether from grief or addiction, my biological father hung himself the next day. And again my adoptive father was involved. I was hungry and trying to make toast when the neighbor smelled smoke and called the fire department. I have a vivid memory of Lou, my adoptive dad, forcing the apartment door open and finding me hiding under the kitchen sink.

Claude's circumstances were entirely different from my experiences. He returned from a doctor's visit, sawed the barrel off a 12 gauge shotgun, crawled into his bathtub, closed the shower curtain and shot himself in the neck. The four of us surmised he must have gotten some really bad news from the doctor.

After the ambulance left we kept daring each other to sneak into the house to have a look at the blood soaked shower enclosure. There were no takers, but out of the four of us, Dagger was the one I thought would actually do it. He was cold for a kid our age, and he routinely accepted dares and accomplished them unscathed. Not this time though, his only concern was what had been done with the shotgun. His buddy, Charlie, was the most vocal while Alvin and I tried to maintain some sense of respect.

"Should've shot the doctor," Charlie proclaimed.

Alvin was not happy with that, he liked to sit on Claude's porch and chat with him and Mrs. Steinbrenner while petting her cat. Alvin was dressed in his cub scout uniform that day, covered in dog hair as usual, the yellow bandana wrapped about his face as if he was going to rob a stagecoach. He had outgrown the uniform, but he loved it anyway.

"What good would that have done?" Alvin was puzzled by Charlie's assertion.

"Doctors are always wrong, and they charge too much, my dad

has never been to a doctor and when I was in the hospital they damn near killed me."

Charlie had been hospitalized with whooping cough a couple years prior, and he still puffed on an inhaler intermittently. His father assigned blame to the doctors, not the fact Charlie wasn't vaccinated.

"He was really smart and he always told really good stories about outer space. He was a scientist." In light of Charlie's theory, Alvin felt it necessary to defend Claude's intelligence.

Claude taught physics at a local college before his retirement. I remember him talking me through changing the antifreeze in his car once, making every step so simple I felt like a mechanic when I was done. We would often do chores for him, everything from cleaning his gutters to weeding his garden. I guess it was the teacher in him that left us always wanting to do more.

"Not so smart if he blew his head off," Charlie continued, "when I was gettin' a haircut the other day this guy was telling the barber if you want to kill yourself you just get soaking wet and go for a long walk in the woods."

"That wouldn't kill you Charlie." My interest had peaked, probably due to my own experiences with suicide.

"I'm telling you what the guy said Noah, he said get soaking wet and go for a long walk in the woods on a real cold day. First you start shiverin', then it stops, then you get real warm, then you take your coat off and lay down for a nap and never wake up – painless."

Claude didn't have any family, and for the most part, no one knew much about him outside of his retirement from the college. In the summer, the neighborhood would get together for a block party and close down Myrtle Avenue. We were on the east side and there was a real ethnic mix. The Italian ladies, the Ukrainian ladies, and the Polish ladies would put on a feast that day while we ran up and down the street, never having to dodge a car once.

At the last block party, as day grew into night, and we were still allowed away from home when the street lights came on, Claude set up a telescope and invited us all to have a look. There was a lunar eclipse that night, and none of us had ever seen one, let alone heard of one. Alvin was glued to the telescope so tightly that Claude had to lift him out of the way so the rest of us could have a look.

Yeah, I thought, this Claude guy is pretty cool, treating us to a lunar eclipse while our fathers parked themselves in front of the keg, swilling one glass of beer after another. That's what made his suicide so hard to accept. He always had something interesting to share, and what he shared was always simple and useful, making perfect sense, and he always appeared happy to be sharing this knowledge with us.

Still, no one really knew a hell of a lot about him, including Mrs. Steinbrenner. Somehow it fell upon her to go through Claude's belongings and give what she could to charity. She was looking for some help, but the only one brave enough to assist was Alvin. The rest of us had been terrorized by a ghost story involving the house now. Someone thought they saw Claude sitting on his front porch and the rumor spread like wildfire.

Alvin was rewarded for his efforts. He walked away with some text books and scientific journals as well as a small jar of change, probably a couple bucks or so, and something he said he was going to share only with me. He pulled a coin out of his pocket, a quarter, and placed it in the palm of his hand so I could see.

"Big deal, it's a quarter."

"Take a look at the date." Alvin smiled and pointed a finger at the palm of his hand.

"Holy shit, 2052, come on it's got to be fake, let me feel it."

"It ain't fake and you ain't touching it." He slid the coin back into his pocket.

I asked to see the coin again from time to time that summer, but

Alvin always refused, asserting it was stolen by time travelers who broke into his house. The same time travelers who were responsible for Claude's death. More tall tales. The older we got, the more unbelievable his tales became. Alvin was never at a loss for spinning yarns, and his conviction while telling them was disturbing. Falsehood after falsehood, a fantastic saga born out of a grain of sand, his trademark.

A CHAT IN THE WALK-IN

CHARLIE COSSACK'S BAR & GRILL
UTICA, NY
1988

Bohdan tapped on the office door before opening it just enough to poke his head in. It was a large head. Bohdan was an immense man, sloppy in appearance and largely unskilled with the English language, but he and his associate Gennady were as loyal as they were massive to their employer Charlie Cossack.

"Yeah, what's up?"

Charlie was just ending a phone call and motioned Bohdan to enter the office.

"Little Ricky wanna' chat in walk-in."

"What the hell does he want now, just loan him the money or extend his tab, tell him I might have some work for him in a few weeks."

"Not about 'dat boss, he lookin' really bad, say he need you help."

"All right, pat him down, we can't be too careful with that private investigator hanging around, I'll get my coat."

Charlie conducted all confidential business in the walk-in cooler. Participants were patted down for electronics and weapons before entering. Adjacent to the cooler was a clothing rack with some assorted sizes of winter coats. A coat was always offered to a participant out of courtesy. The overhead light in the cooler flickered for a few seconds when it was switched on, evolving to a dull yellow when fully illuminated. The cooler itself was anemic in supplies, some frozen hamburger patties, french-fries, and chicken wings on wire rack shelving. In order to get the liquor license, food needed to be dispensed, but Charlie's customers were as a whole more interested in alcohol than dining, especially the daytime denizens.

"So what gives Ricky?"

Charlie was startled by Ricky's appearance. His arm was in a sling, one of the fingers poking out was splinted, and his head was bandaged from front to back, with the bandages stopping just above his eyebrows. A trail of dried blood extended from the bandages down both sides of his face and neck. Must be Ricky and the charming Melissa Mankiller had experienced another night of hard drinking and marital bliss.

"Look at me Charlie, that bitch is going to kill me, just look at me, and it gets worse, the cops arrested me, and when I was released she chased me down the sidewalk in her car, and the cops just stood there laughing – laughing at her driving a fucking car down a city sidewalk."

"So what do you want me to do?"

"She respects you Charlie, just make her stop, she's out to kill me."

"Get Ricky a coat Bohdan, he doesn't need a cold on top of all this."

"I don't need a coat Charlie, I just need her gone."

"I'm not going to hurt your wife, you two have always had a love, hate thing going on, maybe you just need a cooling off period."

"A cooling off period – let me tell you what she did to me last night, she was bitching at me to put the snow tires on her car, when I refused she threw them on top of me when I was laying on the couch, do you know the strength that takes, they were on rims for Christ's sake."

Bohdan broke into laughter. Charlie looked towards Bohdan and nodded in disapproval. Bohdan suppressed his laughter with a slight choke and meandered out of the cooler, disappointed he wouldn't hear more about Ricky's predicament.

"Yeah, really fucking funny huh, she came bustin' through the front door with a tire under each arm, like fuckin' Godzilla stompin' Tokyo, I'm not shitting you, she's out to kill me – she's been looking for me all day."

"So, why did you get arrested, you must have done something."

"I pushed her down the cellar steps when she was chasing me around the house, but that didn't stop her, she was out of control, like a wounded elephant."

"Listen, I'll ask her nicely to stop, maybe offer her a few bucks, have you got a place to stay now until this blows over?"

"At the YMCA until she finds out."

"Let's have a drink on the house before you leave, you need to calm down."

Charlie took his coat off and tucked it under his arm. He walked Little Ricky to the bar with one hand on his shoulder.

"That hurts Charlie."

Ricky winced as he took a seat at the bar. Gennady poured shots of Wild Turkey for all three. Bohdan sat at a nearby table, gazing at a wall mounted television, fixated on his favorite soap opera. All four were oblivious to the entrance of an additional customer.

Gennady's eyes widened as he caught sight of Melissa moving through the front double doors. She was limping, her left leg casted from the knee down, around her neck a plaid scarf, in her arms an aluminum baseball bat, and upon her face a scowl from hell.

Charlie flinched as he felt a rush of air pass by him along with a hum reminiscent of a bumble bee. And then the dull thud and the resulting ping made when the bat located Little Ricky Mankiller's head, dead center on his temple.

Ricky fell from the bar stool and onto the floor, blood trickled from his ear, and an eerie snoring sound emanated from his mouth. Charlie's shot glass fell from his hand and smashed on the floor. Melissa dropped the bat and limped slowly away and out the door, taking a seat on the showcase window sill. She pulled a pack of cigarettes from her sleeveless house coat and lit one up. She dropped her head and began to sob as a light snow started to fall.

Charlie witnessed the trickle of blood from Ricky's ear multiply into a stream as Gennady was frozen in the moment, his mouth wide open. Bohdan remained fixated on the television, taking occasional sips of cola from a bottle he tapped against the table with one hand, a remote control in the other.

"Call a fucking ambulance."

The surprise of it all had created an unusual tenor of desperation in Charlie's voice.

After the medics removed Ricky, Bohdan returned from the utility closet with a mop and bucket. He generously poured bleach into the bucket and began mopping up the pool of blood.

Charlie gave a statement to the police and Melissa was taken away in a patrol car. She never budged from the window sill during the ensuing commotion. The baseball bat was confiscated as evidence and Ricky was pronounced dead at the hospital, leaving Melissa with a murder charge, soon to be reduced to manslaughter in lieu of the couple's history of mutual spousal abuse and violence.

Charlie offered to pay for Melissa's attorney, but she would have none of it.

When asked how she would plead, she stood, pushed the public defender out of the way and barked at the judge.

"I'm guilty your honor, but the little bastard had it coming, believe me."

TIME IS OF THE ESSENCE

THE BAR & GRILL
UTICA, NY
1988

For some reason, maybe out of pity or childhood loyalty, Charlie Cossack had allowed Alvin Bean to receive his mail at the Bar & Grill. And he received a lot of mail. The return addresses were often from government agencies and prestigious universities.

Gennady, who bartended most afternoons when not preoccupied with his boss's other business concerns, delighted in seeing Alvin seated at a booth along with a draft beer, tearing into his mail. Alvin, at times, could be profoundly depressed, but when he was opening his mail, it was always Christmas morning.

Out of respect for the recently departed Alvin, Charlie kept all the incoming mail, thinking someday a next of kin would arrive. Alvin left all his possessions to Charlie in a hand written will, presented to Charlie one day when Alvin was embarrassed he couldn't pay his bar tab.

When Charlie arrived to clean out Alvin's apartment, he found it cluttered with magazines, video tapes, and books. Lots and lots of books. Most of the volumes were in relation to some branch of science or medicine. But he did find the back pack Alvin had specifically mentioned, and the notebooks contained within. All four. Charlie leafed through them, they were full of equations and notes, along with essays on his plans for a better world. This was all meaningless to Charlie, but he decided to store the back pack along with the mail until a family member showed up. But no one ever did. So the back pack and an ever growing bag of mail hung from a hook in the walk-in cooler. Once a day Gennady would stuff any new mail into the bag.

Then, the visitors began to arrive. At first, two men, showing credentials from NASA wandered into the bar, asking about Alvin. It had been a few months since they received letters from him, and they were interested in his whereabouts since all their return correspondence went unanswered.

"Did he threaten you guys, he's been known to do that."

Gennady was taken aback by the arrival of the two, and he doubted their credentials. Most likely Alvin had connected with them at some point during one of his mental health stays.

"No, no threats."

The younger of the two strangers looked about the barroom as his eyes adjusted from the sunny outside to the darkness within. His glasses lightened from the effect.

"Well, unfortunately, he passed away about a year ago, got hit by a car right out front here. Lingered for a while, but he never recovered."

The two men, dressed in business attire, stepped away from the bar and had a brief conversation before engaging Gennady once more. The older of the two initiated the questioning. Gennady noticed a pocket protector full of pens and pencils jutting out from his sports coat, and thought that was a nice touch, maybe the other one would pull out a slide rule. The deeper, more humorous question was, what the hell had Alvin been feeding these two.

"Did he ever mention any notebooks, did he keep any of his writings here, did he live here?"

"No, he didn't live here, the boss let him get his mail here, a lot of the time he would be scribbling away in one of the booths before leaving, but he never left anything here."

"Could we speak to your boss?"

"I guess. Hey Bohdan, go get the boss, will you."

Bohdan grumbled as he stepped away from his lunch and made

his way to Charlie's office.

Charlie returned, perturbed at the interruption.

"Alvin didn't live here, the poor bastard would hang out here, he didn't bother anyone, so I don't think I can help you with anything else."

"Would you happen to know the whereabouts of any notebooks he owned?"

What the hell had Alvin got himself into now, Charlie thought. These two couldn't be who they said they were.

"No notebooks, everything in his apartment went to Good Will, so what do you want with these notebooks?"

"We get a lot of mail, and Alvin had been writing to our public relations department for years, but some equations he recently sent came to the attention of engineering, and we were hoping to speak to him about it."

"Sorry fellas, nothing like that here. I think he's got an aunt in California, you could check with her."

Charlie would never surrender the notebooks to these two, it just didn't smell right. Alvin probably convinced them he was a millionaire and his account numbers were written down somewhere. Weird, but then again, it would be exactly something Alvin would do to get attention.

The two left, visibly disappointed. Gennady looked to Charlie and shrugged his shoulders. Bohdan never looked up from the cheeseburger he was demolishing, pieces of ground beef clung to his moustache.

"What the hell Bohdan, how about a napkin."

Charlie returned to his office, but stopped at the cooler first to grab the back pack. No sense in letting it stay there in case anyone else showed up looking for it. What the hell had Alvin been up to.

A few months later an elderly gentleman entered the bar early one afternoon. He was well dressed and had the aura of money about him. He was accompanied by a much younger woman, who Gennady perceived to be arm candy. The regulars had left for the day and Gennady was dumping ashtrays and wiping down the counter.

"Can I help you?"

"I hope so, would you happen to know an Alvin Bean?"

"Alvin died about a year ago, if you're looking for his notebooks, they're not here, that was just some craziness he invented, he was mentally ill you know."

"Not necessarily looking for notebooks, just him. He proposed some interesting ideas to a neurological clinic I fund, and I was hoping to speak to him about it."

The young woman was completely disinterested. She seated herself at the bar and looked around the place. She appeared uncomfortable with the seedy barroom ambience. She lit a cigarette and let out a sigh. Gennady placed an ashtray in front of her and continued his conversation with her elderly companion.

"Well, he's dead and all his stuff went to Good Will, so I guess you're out of luck."

The elderly gent perceived the accent in Gennady's voice as Eastern European.

"Where are you from, Ukraine, Russia maybe?"

"Nah, you're close though, Belarus."

The old gent leaned forward and whispered something to Gennady in Belarusian. Gennady was impressed with the stranger's mastery and pronunciation of the Belarusian language.

"Would you like to live forever – I might be able to make that happen if you could tell me what you know about Alvin Bean."

"If you told me I could live forever, I wouldn't believe you, and I'm not sure I'd want to. How about a drink?"

Gennady replied in Belarusian, but wondered if the young woman thought they were talking about her. He doubted she could speak the language due to appearance alone. She was Asian, as beautiful as she was bored, not a hair out of place, just the perfect amount of makeup and perfume, nails perfectly manicured, and her scarlet red dress was alluring but not revealing.

"The young woman would like a glass of champagne, and I'd like a pint of the best draft beer you have."

The conversation now returned to English.

"Okay, no champagne, but one Utica Club on the way."

The old man took a sip of his beer and spoke to Gennady in Belarusian once again.

"You see this beautiful woman next to me, I've got maybe a year or two with her before my health sours. Alvin presented us with a way to extend life for a near eternity."

"Like I said, Alvin was no doctor, and he's dead, so you're out of luck."

Gennady answered in English. He always thought it rude to speak a language to one and not all, although the young woman didn't seem to resent the linguistics she had been subjected to.

The old gent replied in kind.

"His solution wasn't a miracle drug, it was a brain implant – he designed the implant, but he never finished his work on where and how to place the implant in the brain."

"Are you sure we're talking about the same Alvin, he had all he could do to ride a bicycle."

"Listen, it's not about time, it's about the individual's perception of time. The insert, when placed, and it has to be precise, will make minutes seem like decades, years will stretch into eons. It's based on a child's concept of time, it's so simple it's elegant. Time is merely an experience, and it is different for everyone on the planet, it's as unique as a fingerprint or a snowflake."

"You're really starting to creep me out. Like I told you, Alvin is dead and all his bullshit died with him."

The young woman rubbed her cigarette out as the old man took one last gulp of his draft beer.

"If you find anything or remember someone who might know something, you let me know."

The old man stood and dropped a one hundred dollar bill on the bar. There was a phone number written on the bill. His companion took his arm as they made their way to the front double doors.

"Okay, but you're barking up the wrong tree here."

Gennady took a quick look at the phone number and pocketed the bill. Boy, Alvin may have been insane, but he sure was one of a kind. Wait until Charlie hears this one.

DON'T LET THE BEDBUGS BITE

CORNELL UNIVERSITY
ITHACA, NY
1987

Dr. Libby Clearwater agreed to meet with a potential study participant after multiple phone calls and messages from him. The study was officially closed now, but an opening had developed after the loss of one study member due to a motor vehicle accident.

Noah Gregory was a Captain in the Utica Fire Department and she thought that alone might add insight to the study in terms of unusual sleep patterns and sleep deprivation. Firefighters held a job in which employees are allowed to sleep, but also mandated to respond from full sleep to a state of mental acuity in seconds. Captain Gregory reported a history of sleep walking as a child, and claimed to have on and off experiences with lucid dreaming. Two topics of interest to be addressed in the study.

"So, Captain Gregory, tell me how you learned of the study."

Libby was reviewing Noah's questionnaire. He certainly had checked the right boxes to pique her interest.

"Your cousin Naomi, she's bartending at a place I go to once in a while and somehow we got onto the subject of dreams."

"I haven't spoken to her in quite some time, but it sounds like our mothers must still be in touch."

Admittedly, Libby hadn't kept in touch with most of her family, she had been consumed with getting her doctorate in clinical psychology, and this study was to bear the fruits of that hard work. But her family, due to their Native American Heritage, did place an interest in dreaming most cultures wouldn't understand. This interest derived from folklore and spirituality.

"You say in the questionnaire your lucid dreaming evolved from the enjoyable to the troublesome, could you explain that in more detail?"

"I'll share this with you, but you're going to think it's weird. It went from knowing I was dreaming and doing anything I wanted like jumping over buildings to having some very disturbing conversations with friends and family and not being able to wake up."

"That doesn't sound weird, really, I don't think it's anything out of the ordinary."

"Yeah, but these people I'm talking to are all dead, and it doesn't stop until they tell me they're done talking. It usually starts with a knock on the door, and when I open it there they are, and they aren't looking so good, but each time I open the door they look a little better until they finally go away, but until they do it's super stressful to fall asleep, it all seems so real."

"So how have you been dealing with the stress related to this – have you sought counseling of any type?"

"I've been self medicating for years, no counseling or doctors. If the fire department was to find out I was seeing a psychiatrist along with my other injuries, they'd pension me off. I can't afford that with an ex-wife and kid. Ironic, huh? They'd rather have an alcoholic on the job rather than someone getting help for mental issues."

"An alcohol problem – that alone will disqualify you from the study."

"It's been the only thing that seems to help – I've got all the initials, I know that for a fact."

"The initials?"

"You know, PTSD, OCD, AA meetings, I've got them all, some of them from my job, I've met a lot of good people who didn't deserve to be dead, and my childhood, which I just can't seem to shake, so I've been drinking it away, on and off for years."

"I'm sorry Noah, I don't think you'd be a good fit for the study, but I can recommend you to some colleagues who may be able to help you."

"I don't want to be in the study, I was asked to come here to tell you something. Have you ever heard of the Veryovkina Cave?"

Libby grew uneasy with Noah's responses. She feared he may be on the cusp of a psychological emergency. Some more questioning was necessary to determine if he was capable of harming himself. That appeared to be the crisis, although his calmness during the interview alleviated that concern at present.

"No, I'm not familiar with that cave, or any other cave for that matter, why are you?"

"Well, I never heard of it either until I was told about it in a dream by this guy I knew as a kid who's in a coma now."

"So, this cave actually exists?"

"Yeah, I looked it up, it's the world's deepest cave, somewhere around Russia, and this guy who keeps telling me about it, wants me to tell you to tell the scientists here about it."

"Tell them what?"

"He says there is a shaft in this cave that has never been explored, and at the bottom of that shaft is an underground lake and at the bottom of that lake is something which has been collecting sub-atomic particles for millions of years. I have no idea what that means, but he's been pleading with me to tell you, and if I do, he says he'll go away. For good."

"Well, you've done just that, how do you feel now?"

Obviously, Noah believed what he was saying, and it was always disturbing to speak to someone so committed to a delusion.

"I feel relieved, sort of like having a drink or two, maybe I can get back to normal now since I've delivered the message."

"I hope so too Noah, but let me give you some referrals before you leave, some people who might be able to make you feel even better, even without the alcohol."

Noah took the list of referrals Libby laid on the table and pocketed them before shaking Libby's hand and thanking her again for taking the time to listen to him.

Noah muttered to himself as he pulled out of the campus parking lot to begin his journey home.

"You promised Alvin, leave me alone, just leave me the fuck alone now."

That evening, Libby took a valium before getting into bed. Most of her interest in the sleep study was that she had an incredibly tough time falling asleep and staying asleep, and she could never remember dreaming, not one memory of dreaming in her entire life to date. She envied those who fell into REM sleep and could stay there for hours. What a gift she thought as her mind wandered through the interview she had conducted with Captain Gregory, his experiences were not a gift though, they seemed torturous.

Alvin Bean stepped into Libby's mind that evening to deliver the first lucid dream of her existence. He manifested himself to appear as a young man, dressed as a traffic patrolman, a whistle hanging from a lanyard around his neck.

Libby looked from the mountain where they both stood onto a village below. It felt like a clear fall day with the sun directly overhead. She turned for a panoramic view of her surroundings when she spotted Alvin, and thought it peculiar a policeman would be wearing unlaced tennis shoes. He beckoned her towards the mouth of a cave with broad sweeping motions, his white gloves sparkling in the sunlight, as if motioning a vehicle through an intersection. She walked towards him and seated herself upon a large boulder placed there from an earlier excavation.

"Are you the man Captain Gregory told me about?"

"I'm Alvin Bean, Noah and I were friends all the way through school, although most of the time he thought of me as a nuisance, but he always listened to me."

"A nuisance?"

"Yeah, I had some issues, but they're gone now, but I need to show you something fascinating."

Alvin placed a pen light in his mouth, the only illumination for them both as he took Libby's hand. They floated into the cave opening and through a labyrinth of tunnels until they reached their destination. Alvin held the pen light above his head and the entire cavern, adorned in crystals, beamed with light all around them, revealing the lake Noah spoke about.

The water was calm and dark with an occasional splash made by creatures living in it, now sensing an outside presence.

"This cave connects with many others and self ventilates, like an underground transit system does."

Alvin was elated to be sharing this with someone who might finally appreciate his discovery.

"Why am I here Alvin, what do you want me to do?"

"There are those out there who view this as nothing more than a hole in the ground, they plan to use it as a dump for radioactive waste, and I'm unsure what that will do to whatever is at the bottom of this lake. It may kill it, it may supercharge it, I don't know, but I do know neither of those scenarios would be good for the planet. Trust me."

"It's alive?"

"I'm not sure what it is, but I do know it's been here for millions of years, it could be an intelligent bacteria for all I know, or some form of artificial intelligence, I just need to find out why it's here and for what purpose."

Libby caught sight of her reflection in the dark waters of the lake. She was garbed in a white lab coat, her hair pulled behind her ears into a pony tail. The small stud earrings she wore were spinning furiously, obviously from some magnetic force in the cave.

"This isn't the healthiest place to be for any extended period of time," Alvin explained, "the force in that lake is flipping the ions in our bodies much like an MRI scan does, only thousands of times more powerful."

"Alvin, this isn't my field, who do you want me to tell?"

"There's a professor at Cornell who just completed a paper on quarks and neutrinos, Cyrill Kwon, tell him, but do me a favor, don't mention any of this to Noah, he'll be getting some bad news in a few days about a biopsy, and I promised him if he spoke to you, I'd leave him alone."

Libby nodded her head in agreement as Alvin clicked the pen light off, plunging the cavern into darkness.

"Good night, sleep tight, and don't let the bedbugs bite."

That was a rhyme Libby's mother always told her when she would hop into bed as a little girl, now delivered by a cryptic visitor with a strange request.

Libby awoke to the buzzing of her alarm clock. A full night's sleep and, to her amazement, a dream, a vivid, lucid dream. She could remember every detail. The cave, quarks, neutrinos, Cyrill Kwon. She'd need to check the staff directory for that name, but somehow she knew it would be there. There must be a purpose to this, it was all just too odd not to have merit.

Libby sat on the edge of the bed, cupping her face with both hands and wondered how a rhyme delivered by a parent to a child about being bitten by bugs could be soothing, but it was. She sighed and rose to her feet.

"And what in the hell is a quark?"

FUCK ME LIKE YOU HATE ME (A LOVE STORY)

A HUNTING CABIN
MASSENA, NY
1988

Hannigan Butler was duct taped to a folding chair, wearing nothing but a pair of boxer briefs. Next to him was Wendy, his enabler, fellow addict, and lover. She too was duct taped to a folding chair, clad only in a bra and panties.

It was bitter cold. Wendy was shaking uncontrollably and each breath Hannigan took was razor sharp. In front of them stood Charlie Cossack, dressed for the weather with a heavy coat, ski cap, and gloves. Charlie's associate, Gennady, stood behind Hannigan and Wendy. At different intervals during the questioning he would pour water over them from a plastic bucket he had filled in the cabin. The frigid air was so cold, water poured from the bucket took on the appearance of snow.

Charlie's cohort, Bohdan, was further from the foursome, starting a chain saw he had brought with him, a shovel laid at his feet. Bohdan and Gennady were immense in size, almost cartoonish in a sinister way. Gennady had dragged the seated captives to the surface of the frozen pond, where all five were now located. It was a clear night sky with a full moon, headlights from the vehicles at the cabin cast shadows upon the ice.

Hannigan was thinking the saw might be for dismembering them, the shovel may be for burial, but the ground was much too frozen for that. Then it became clear, Bohdan was cutting a hole in the frozen pond and using the shovel to pry the blocks of ice out.

"It's your choice," Charlie continued, "tell me what I want to know and you can die painlessly, or Butler, you can watch that fucking skank next to you go first, because we both know she doesn't give a flying fuck about you, so killing you first would be an abject, fucking waste of time, right?"

Hannigan didn't respond, but he knew Charlie was correct.

Wendy was cruel, selfish, and a compulsive liar, but then again, all addicts carried that gene, but she surely had perfected the self indulgence and manipulation it takes to keep the habit going while still maintaining a high degree of functionality.

Hannigan's teeth were chattering, his extremities were numb. Wendy whimpered, finally breaking into speech after Gennady once again poured icy water over her head.

"I told them you kept drugs and money in the walk-in, I was pissed off at you after you fired me again."

Wendy struggled to get the words out, each word spit out while at the same time gasping for a breath, her complexion now a pale blue.

"Well that's a first Butler, your slut girlfriend didn't try to pin it on you."

Three meth dealers had set fire to Charlie's bar in Utica on a lethargic Friday night. And to add insult to injury they used the support anchoring one of Charlie's bird feeders in the alley to ram open the rear office door before rolling in a small tank of propane wrapped in blasting caps. That bird feeder was visited by orioles every summer. It had taken years to attract them to the feeder, in an alley of all places, and using the feeder support to smash open the door was more upsetting to Charlie than any fire.

It was a provocation fire, they had no intention of a robbery, their goal was to send the message they were acquiring territory, and Charlie was in their way. They had to be users as well, meth makes for profound irrationality and rage. Otherwise, they would have known Charlie would hunt them down and exact a painful revenge, but Wendy had spoken what she believed to be the truth to protect Hannigan, and Charlie thought this interesting. Maybe she wasn't completely without decency as he had thought.

Hannigan was slipping into a dream state, just as Charlie had warned. First you shiver and become disoriented, then you warm up and fall asleep. Forever. It was happening all right, just as predicted.

"Okay, you fucking degenerates, here's your choices – Wendy, you take the cash and bus ticket I'll give you, you find a place to live wherever that ticket takes you, and every Friday you call the number on that ticket. If I don't hear from you on any given Friday, someone shows up at your door and puts a bullet in your head, or you can take a dip in the pond and do everybody a fucking favor."

Charlie's voice grew louder and his speech was unnecessarily peppered with expletives. He needed his prisoners to believe everything he said, even if he did not. When you corner someone, they have the ability to become your most ardent enemy, and once they see a threat unfulfilled, they have the upper hand. Hopefully, this intimidation and the mercy to follow will be the proper dose of manipulation, no more, no less.

Wendy shook her head in agreement, hoping Charlie was telling the truth.

"And as for you, Hannigan Butler, Treasury Agent and all around drunken piece of shit, I've got a job for you out west. You'll be on a plane tomorrow morning with one of my associates, and if I don't hear from you every Friday, the sack of venereal disease sitting next to you eats a bullet – or go for a swim, what do you say?"

Hannigan mustered the physicality to whisper, "I'll be on the plane."

Charlie had good use for Hannigan. With the experience he had as a Treasury Agent, he was just the guy to supervise an operation Charlie was establishing in Nevada.

The scene on the ice was pure theater. Word had spread about Wendy and Hannigan's relationship, and the fire was just the lever Charlie needed to pressure Hannigan Butler into running his new enterprise. The bar meant nothing to Charlie, no one was killed and the place was over insured, besides, the move to Buffalo had been underway for a couple months. A win, win, win.

Bohdan had alerted Charlie to Wendy and Hannigan. He was suspicious of Hannigan and the attention he was paying to Wendy, occupying a seat, front row and center any time she was bartending, and drinking for free through Wendy's sleight of hand at the cash register. An offense she was terminated for.

Wendy had worked for Charlie at a strip club down the street from the bar, but she was drugging customers and stealing wallets to support her habit. At times it wasn't beyond her to pleasure customers after hours if the price was right, and the price always depended on how much her addiction was suffering at the moment. Charlie fired her under no uncertain terms, but he later swallowed her sob story and let her bartend at the Bar & Grill, under the supervision of Bohdan.

Hannigan Butler had arrived in Utica a few months earlier to investigate a fire at a nursing facility Charlie was a silent partner in. The circumstances surrounding the fire were bizarre, and somehow the Catholic Church had hired Butler to downplay the rumors circulating about the fire actually being a miracle.

The mystery was, did Butler just wander into the Bar & Grill, or did he have any inside information on who actually owned the facility, and the fraud going on there. Charlie enlisted his attorney, Bonita Romero, to do some digging while at the same time making sure the welcome mat was always rolled out for the drunken private investigator.

Bonita assured Charlie that Butler no longer had any ties with the Treasury Department, he had burned all his bridges there, and any chance of him digging up information on Charlie's finances, was at best, remote. He had fallen under the sway of Wendy's charms, as hard as that was to fathom, but then again, misery loves company.

"You guys all fall into the same trap, the enemy complex trap."

Bonita and Charlie were seated at a coffee shop a few storefronts across the street from the burned out remains of the Bar & Grill. They watched the Fire Marshals sift through the rubble from their vantage point.

"What's that mean?"

"It's what keeps you motivated, right? Find the enemy, destroy the enemy, all the while creating enemies – and by creating enemies you create more problems for yourself."

Charlie sat back and digested her observations. She might be right. According to Bonita, this Butler guy was an expert in detecting counterfeit money and how it was laundered, he could certainly use him. Charlie had recently been accepting piles of counterfeit bills in exchange for brokering drug deals and weapon sales. He needed a smooth way to move the money, and the casinos in Nevada, along with a crew supervised by Butler, might be just the ticket.

"As I see it Charlie, you've only got one real enemy, and that's the lunatic in Toronto we work for. We need to be careful, that son-of-a-bitch is as smart as he is vicious."

Charlie nodded in agreement. His sidelining of cash and deals was getting too big to keep under wraps for much longer.

"How's the place in South America coming?"

Charlie slid an ashtray across the table to Bonita.

"It's about ready for us, but you've got some cleaning up to do around here before we make any moves."

The next afternoon, Bohdan and Gennady visited Wendy at her apartment. Hannigan was there as well, and they both had been smoking crack prior to the arrival of the two box cars standing before them.

"Get dressed, we go for ride," Bohdan delivered the orders while Gennady covered the couples' mouths with duct tape.

The foursome paused at the bottom of the stairs as Gennady took a quick look around before he deposited the couple into the back seat of a stretch limo. Charlie had driven to the cabin a few hours prior to the apprehension.

On the way, Hannigan tried to comfort Wendy by nodding his head affirmatively, as if he could make this all better, but he knew he couldn't. And although he did love her, he did not trust her. Addiction is steeped in fear and weakness, it is self-survival at its ugliest.

Hannigan's memory drifted to the first time he had spent the night with Wendy. After three shots of tequila and two lines of cocaine, Wendy made sure her apartment door was locked as she grabbed a three ring notebook lying on the coffee table where they had lined the cocaine.

"I've written a poem for you Hannigan, I call it 'Fuck Me Like You Hate Me'. "

And Hannigan complied, because, although he could never hate her, he could gladly fulfill the self loathing her poem implied.

SLOW MOTION KUNG-FU BOXING

THE WHITE CARDINAL RANCH
PATAGONIA, SOUTH AMERICA
1993

Lili-Che Faithful feared the approach of this day ever since Charlie's diagnosis. Crushing bad news followed by denial, leading to a second, third, and fourth opinion, with ensuing therapies and medication cocktails, all to no avail. Specialists flown in from all over the world, experts in their respective fields of medicine, paid exorbitant amounts of money to develop treatments, under the not so subtle warnings to keep Charlie Cossack's condition and location a secret.

Charlie had slipped into unconsciousness after being moved to the Intensive Care Unit at the ranch. The unit was housed in what was once a library and billiards room. Within a week, Lili-Che had the room re-organized, staff hired, and her own bed and personal effects moved there.

But the time had come. The pain had become so severe, Charlie was medicated to near suffocation before it became bearable. This evening, Lili-Che was to say her good-byes to Charlie, her lover, friend, confidante, and savior.

They met in junior high school, the attraction between them went far beyond teenage love, obsession or infatuation. After the car accident, they were to be separated for nearly twenty years, until a random encounter set the stage for the re-ignition of their love affair.

By then, Charlie was a well established insurance scam artist, his exploits into drug and weapon sales were legendary in the criminal community, yet he maintained a low profile as a bar owner and strip club entrepreneur. These businesses only existed to show losses, while he moved millions of dollars through them for his venture capitalist, a powerful and sadistic man based in Toronto. Charlie would only refer to him as Uncle Roman.

Lili's life had taken some unusual paths after the car accident. Her family – mother, father, and brother were killed. She was moved from Utica to a trauma center in Albany. Her condition was grave, but her recovery, according to the physicians there, was nothing short of miraculous. But she was left with some burdens in exchange for her life. Among them, severe memory loss and no sense of smell or taste. She ate only out of necessity, not hunger, and the headaches were at times crippling. What she knew of the years before the accident were only momentary flashbacks, no matter how hard she tried to recall, the memories brought forth were scant and probably based on the stories her grandmother told her.

After the death of her grandmother, Lili married and had a child, a beautiful daughter named Sofia. The marriage, however, was not beautiful. The husband was a cheater and a drug abuser. After several beatings, orders of protections, and arrests, the husband found himself in an upstate New York prison after a failed robbery attempt at a 24 hour gas station convenience store.

Lili found work at a grocery store and an apartment through friends of her grandmother. An aging couple who took it upon themselves to watch over her as an obligation to the dear friend they had known and loved.

It wasn't until Charlie brought a suitcase full of money to his strip club in Albany that he saw Lili-Che again. There she was dancing on stage. It was a gut wrenching epiphany of what might have been. Charlie never gave a thought to fate, luck, divine intervention, or predestination. They were words that meant nothing to him. He was determined to create his own destiny, he would forge his own path, he would carve his way through the jungle with the biggest machete he could find, and he would chop down anyone or anything that got in his way.

After all, he had done well for himself, and he could only thank healthy cynicism for that. Luck was not responsible for his gains. Intelligence and suspicion had brought him this far, but now he heard a knock at the door he would eagerly answer. He would open the door, the door that had been slammed shut some twenty years ago, but it would take planning and patience, two attributes Charlie had been cultivating since grade school.

Lili slid her chair up to Charlie's hospital bed. The ventilator tubing had been removed along with the IV lines. The cardiac monitor was running, but the alarm was silenced. Lili would look to it when the time came and a doctor would be summoned to concur Charlie had died. His breathing was shallow, a slight rise and fall of his chest and a faint wheeze echoed from his nostrils. His thick head of hair had been reduced to thin patches about his scalp, his face showed a day's worth of beard growth, and he was now so emaciated his form barely lifted the sheet covering him. He was no longer recognizable as the man he once was.

Lili pressed her lips against Charlie's ear and gently caressed his arm.

"Charlie, I know you can hear me, it's alright to let go now, it's alright to move on, I'll be okay, Sofia will be okay, Bohdan will be just fine. I promise you the people here on the ranch will be well taken care of."

Tears were streaming down Lili's face. She wiped them along with her nose on a tissue which had been crumpled in her free hand.

"Go on ahead Charlie, find a nice place for us, a place where we can be happy, a place where Sofia can visit, a peaceful place, build it for me just as you assembled this ranch, but I need to tell you something first."

Lili swallowed hard, choking back her tears and apprehensions.

"Remember those letters you wrote to me before I remembered who you were, the errands you sent me on? You did some beautiful things for some desperate people, I know you meant to atone through this, and I'm sure you did, but there's something else you need to do before you leave me. You need to forgive the people you hurt out of some misguided philosophy of revenge and retribution –

you did bad things to some bad people, but that doesn't make it right, ask them now for forgiveness, and forgive them too, please promise me, please."

Lili laid her head upon Charlie's chest and listened to each respiration as the intervals between them lengthened and their fullness dissipated.

Charlie's mind was awash in memories, some joyful, some disgraceful. The acts of violence and avarice he had become addicted to now disgusted him. Revenge only begets revenge, violence only begets violence, and avarice only begets the worst in us. Can it be so simple as to say you're sorry, can it be that simple he thought.

Within an instant, his mind drifted to a summer in his youth, a summer that felt endless, a summer shared with some boyhood pals, long before any of them developed affinities for women, booze, power, or violence.

This had been a wonderful time in his life, a time when raging hormones were months away, a time when tossing a baseball or watching black and white TV re-runs translated into tranquility and happiness, a time when waiting at the corner store for a delivery of baseball cards or comic books generated butterflies in the stomach excitement.

Getting up the courage to ride a bicycle no handed, and finally doing so with eyes closed, was an incomparable act of bravery. That was the summer Charlie and his pals talked their fathers into giving them Mohawk haircuts. Most of the neighborhood laughed at them, but those haircuts made them unique, it gave them a colossal prestige in their hearts and minds.

And then there was a game Alvin invented, a genius of a game he called Slow Motion Kung-Fu Boxing. He had long been a fan of martial arts, and he had been watching a TV series in which one of the stars was a Kung-Fu master.

But it wasn't about beating each other senseless, it was about taking the punch, taking the kick, all in slow motion with each of their sound effects interjected. They spent many a day that summer perfecting their techniques. Alvin could even delay his speech and mouth movements to resemble a dubbed foreign film. Still in all, Dagger wasn't much of a fan. He may have been maturing faster than the rest of them, or it just wasn't in his nature to accept a punch to the face or a kick to the stomach, slow motion or not.

Noah, the most athletic out of the four, could actually raise a foot to a foe's nose and hold it there, all done in slow motion. Once in a while a punch or kick would slip, and for a brief moment, tempers would flare, but all was forgiven over a bottle of soda and a bag of chips.

So odd, Charlie thought, these are my last thoughts, thoughts about Dagger who died of kidney failure in a California prison, Alvin who was run over by a car and laid in a coma for nearly a year before his death, and Noah, who made it to the minor leagues only to be defeated by injury and alcoholism, and falsely imprisoned for my benefit.

Lili-Che jerked upwards and looked at the cardiac monitor, a straight line, she broke into sobs of disbelief.

"No," she screamed, "no, no, no, please Jesus forgive him."

Charlie could hear her screams, but he was powerless to console her. He now stood in front of a large bay window within a log lined cabin. Next to him stood Lili-Che and Sofia, all three hand in hand. There were Christmas lights around the window and a Christmas tree next to a piano. It was early evening and the Christmas lights filled the room with a palpable sense of comfort. Charlie had never felt such serenity. Beyond the window there was the lake and a dock. The yard, surrounded by a break wall, was illuminated by a flood light shining upon it and the dock. A heavy snow was falling and in the yard there were four boys bundled for the weather, four boys perfecting the art of Slow Motion Kung-Fu Boxing.

THERE ARE NO ENDINGS, ONLY BEGINNINGS

THE PRESENT
THE FUTURE
THE PAST

As of this precise second, I am imploring you to proceed with extreme caution, and if you are suffering from emotional fragility, heart disease, or you have indulged in recreational drugs on a regular basis, please do not continue. The mere attempt will have a severe impact on your mental and physical health. As the saying goes, what you don't know can't hurt you. However, at best, it only saves you the anxiety predestination brings.

For the rest of you, I feel it incumbent on me to inform you that your sense-of-self is in peril, for inevitably it will collapse upon itself and take the universe as you know it, with it. You and I, and everything we have ever known will implode, leaving us as the lonely molecules we once were. Yes, we will fade into the atoms, neutrons, and protons that began it all, in a wilderness of thoughts, emotions, and darkness – a consciousness we once shared, a preamble to all we have ever known. A cyclical nothingness, a nothingness we have experienced before and will experience again and again.

How soon you want to know, how soon before the fear sets in, how soon before the loneliness consumes us? I won't tell you, there is no sense in telling you. What does it matter if it's seconds or hours? Weeks or years? But when it happens, it will happen sooner than any of us would have bargained for. The pages of this book will dissolve in front of your eyes sooner than you can finish this sentence. Your home will disappear piece by piece, each framing member and shingle vanishing in the exact opposite order they were installed.

There will come options, there will come choices, and decisions will have to be made from our cosmic purgatory. Some of you will spend eons voyaging through a new universe, witnessing the birth of stars, planets, and civilizations. Others will seek new life on new worlds. But still others will demand answers, they will scream, "Why?" into the dawning of a new light, a light gaining in brightness and warmth.

Some will choose to re-appear in the exact moment they left our present reality, with the same form, the same mind and personality, and this, the same book in front of them, trying to digest the warning they were given, but now dismiss as the ramblings of an escapist, a silly man desperately trying to mold his fantasies into art.

For me, I will choose to exist solely within the pages you now hold, my only hope being you will join me here.

DONOVAN OTTO'S GREAT ESCAPE

SYRACUSE UNIVERSITY HOSPITAL OF MENTAL HEALTH
SYRACUSE, NY
1969

Alvin Bean had been committed to in-patient care at a Syracuse mental health facility. This would be his first such stay, but not his last. And as strange as it sounds, out of boredom or curiosity, he would mimic symptoms to achieve subsequent stays.

It wasn't for the blend of anti-depressants and psychotropic drugs he was fed, but solely for the fellowship of another patient he had met there. Professor Donovan Otto.

Alvin found Professor Otto fascinating. He always dressed in a white, three-piece suit, a cigarette holder, minus the cigarette, held between his thumb and forefinger, a timepiece attached to his vest pocket by a gold chain, and a fresh red rose pinned to his lapel. Just above his upper lip was a pencil thin moustache, almost unnoticeable, and on any given day he would marvel Alvin with tales of space travel, time travel, immortality, telepathy, and the mysterious workings of the subconscious mind. Alvin was awestruck by Otto's prophesies. Everything from the exact time and date of freak storms to the morning newspaper's headlines. Otto described himself as a genius, and a prophet, and now Alvin's mentor. Loneliness, Alvin thought, is a greater crippler than Polio, but now, upon the arrival of Otto, the solitude was gone.

A few days after their first meeting, Otto confided in Alvin about a plan to escape the facility once and for all. At first Alvin thought this strange because Professor Otto appeared to have full reign over the ward, with the exception of the exit doors. He appeared wary of them, always keeping his distance from them, while at the same time staring intently at the mechanisms which secured them.

"They stay locked, even if there's a fire," Otto whispered to Alvin over lunch one day.

"The orderlies have to verify there's a fire before they'll let us out, if we're still alive that is. And speaking of orderlies, I'd like you to do me a favor concerning the big one, the one they call Hoss."

"He's the mean one, right?"

"Downright cruel – we need to do something about him."

Alvin tacitly nodded his approval to Otto, but there was something Alvin needed to know before accepting the assignment.

"How come you're the only adult in this ward, and how come you only talk to me?"

"You haven't figured it out yet – I'm amazed Beanie, you're a smart kid, don't you realize you're the only one who can see me?"

It made sense now, Alvin thought, just a hallucination probably made more vivid by the amount of drugs being pumped into him. It could be sprinkled into the food here as well. As if there wasn't already enough despair in this place, now a new reason to curl up into a ball and weep.

"I know what you're thinking Alvin, your illness is worsening, but that's not the case, listen to me and I can get you out of here. First of all, stop responding to me verbally, they've been watching you do that."

Alvin nervously liquefied a small cup of Jello by stirring it with a spoon. His hamburger was left uneaten on his tray. Nausea had replaced all hope of leaving the facility any earlier. But Otto's advice did make sense. If he wanted to get out, he'd have to pretend he was getting better. Step one: Stop talking to the invisible man by his side.

"You're catching on now, aren't you – good, but before I get you out of here, we need to discuss the problem of Hoss."

Alvin stared straight ahead to where a nurse stood with a clip board, adjacent to her stood Hoss, viewing the cafeteria for any signs of trouble. He was a big man and delighted in tossing around any of the patients who acted up even for a second. A pale man with a crew cut, tattoos of anchors and ships on his forearms. So strange that his voice didn't match his frame. He spoke in squeaky half sentences, almost childlike. Must be a Navy vet thought Alvin, but a sadist regardless.

"I'm going to show you how to make a blow-gun and a projectile that will render Hoss useless, in the chaos I'll make my escape, but you'll have to listen to me, my every word, and along the way I'll show you how to convince everyone here you're completely well. Just nod if you approve, which I'm sure you will."

A blow gun, now that's interesting. Alvin had seen them advertised in sporting magazines and he had read how tribes in the Amazon have used them for centuries and continue to do so. But, a poison dart, or one capable of taking down Hoss, that would be a stretch to do here under the watchful eyes of the medical and security staffs. And Professor Otto, there's a better than average chance he's just a delusion, but he has been the one beacon of happiness in this prison of fear and depression. Might as well see where this leads.

Under the tutelage of Otto, Alvin learned to pocket medications under his tongue and later hide them within the hollow tubular leg of the folding chair in his room. He would need to mix them at some point to brew the paralytic that would bring down Hoss. As for the blow gun itself, Otto instructed him to unscrew a spindle on his bed board, which when removed, revealed an eighteen inch cylinder with a cavity the size of a dime running through it. The perfect amount of resistance for the projectile he would launch into Hoss's neck.

As for the projectile, the nursing staff would empty used syringes into a sharps container mounted near the nursing station. It was most often overfull. An easy mark, the only danger was being stuck by an unsheathed needle. Just the needle and the hub it screwed into, the paralytic would be forced into the hub until the needle wept, the liquid secured with a small piece of tape. Ingenious, Alvin thought, this Otto is a remarkable thinker, every detail planned to perfection.

"At night, you'll need to practice assembling the blow gun and loading the dart, empty of course. Every chance you get take the deepest breaths you can and practice exhaling to the fullest with your lips pursed, to simulate the blow gun. I estimate you can drive that needle at least an inch into the soft of his neck."

Alvin was seated in the cafeteria. He covered his mouth with a napkin, and turned his head a few inches away from the Professor.

"So how am I supposed to sneak up on him, we're locked in our rooms after ten o'clock every night?"

"Once you're competent and confident with assembling the blow gun and using it, I'll show you a simple trick to open your door, I'd do it for you, but locked doors my young friend, are my kryptonite."

Practice began every night after lights out when patient rooms were secured. Taking apart the bed board, loading the dart, unarmed of course, breathing exercises, and the disassembly of the blow gun and re-assembly of the chair leg and bed board spindle. The paralytic was a mix of three of Alvin's medications along with a thimble full of water supplied by the glass on his night table. These medications were for oral consumption only, racing them into the blood stream was extremely dangerous, but necessary according to Otto's instructions. The last details to be addressed were the locked door and the exact time and date of the mission. Very important details which began to weigh on Alvin. His worries were evident.

"My dear Beanie, the simplest of any number of possible solutions is always the correct one."

Otto shared this scientific principle of economy over breakfast to an attentive Alvin Bean.

"You have been allowed writing paper and plastic tape in your room, and that my friend is the simplest of answers. Apply the tape over the door latch, in a vertical fashion of course, so it cannot be observed, and then fold up enough paper to wedge the door closed. When staff goes door knocking after lights out, it will appear locked, simple enough – right?"

Alvin tucked his head towards his tray and whispered, making sure to avoid the stares of the duty nurse and Hoss.

"I guess so, but when?"

"This Wednesday at midnight. Hoss works the third shift twice a month on a Wednesday. He comes in at eleven, he'll stroll down the hallway with his Polaroid camera checking doors, but he's only interested in one door, and when he gets to that point, you'll strike silently, like a Ninja."

"So, I sneak behind him and shoot the dart – how long for this stuff to work, what if he chases me.?"

"By the time he yanks the dart out of his neck, he'll be hitting the floor, just remember to take the dart with you, lock yourself back into your room, and put everything back like you've been practicing."

"I just hope you're right, I'll never get out of here if I'm caught."

"You won't be, I can assure you, and once I grab the keys from Hoss, I'll be out of here too."

The mission proceeded like clockwork. Alvin tip-toed behind Hoss, a good six feet behind, he had removed his shoes, only socks on his feet, and as soon as Hoss slid the key into the lock mechanism of the door, the dart was launched. As forecasted, Hoss pulled the dart from his neck as he tumbled to the floor. The key was still in the lock, the cylinder had not yet been turned.

Alvin retrieved the dart and was startled by the face at the wire reinforced door window. A young girl, dimly illuminated by the hall night lights, thin, with dark circles under her eyes, greasy blonde hair, shoulder length, and a vacuous stare upon her face.

Alvin rushed back to his room, his socks slid on the floor and he dropped the blow gun. He picked it up, and frantically checked for any other evidence he might have left behind. None in sight, good, he removed the tape from the latch on his door and re-assembled the chair leg and bed frame. He fell upon the bed and wiped the sweat from his eyes and questioned himself out loud as he so often did.

"Just a dream maybe, I hope so, please just let this all be a bad dream."

Alvin wanted to wake and exhale, realizing it was all a dream, pure imagination, but it was not.

He was startled in the early morning by the shriek of the nursing supervisor. She had gone looking for Hoss and found him lying unconscious in the hallway. Then came the ambulance and the medics, and the frantic loading of Hoss onto a stretcher. The nurse followed the stretcher and medics, the Polaroid camera in her hand.

The next morning, Alvin was surprised to see Professor Otto pacing in front of the exit doors in the cafeteria. After a minute or two he stopped and seated himself next to Alvin.

"Well Beanie, it seems I have to add keys to my list of inabilities, couldn't get near enough to them to yank them out of the door lock, so I guess it's back to the drawing board."

"What about Hoss, I saw them wheel him out of here is he okay?"

"That depends on your definition of okay, he's on life support, doesn't look good, guess I overestimated the dosage, my bad, but I thought they'd find him sooner anyway."

Alvin was stunned, he could feel breakfast trying to escape through his throat and mouth.

"Not your fault Beanie, it's all on me. Guess I better get used to not getting out of here. Listen, I'm going to leave you alone for a while, hear you're due to get out soon, but you know where to find me in the future if I reach out, and I just might."

Otto walked away, his appearance grew fainter with each step. Alvin held his head between both hands until he heard someone set a tray down in front of him. Unusual he thought, in the two weeks he's been here, no one had come near him, just like junior high school, a pariah even in juvenile psych.

"Hi Beanie, want my eggs?"

It was the girl at the window last night and she was forcing a smile, a small crack of a smile, a painful smile.

THE CHALLENGE

ST. ANTHONY'S ACADEMY
UTICA, NY
1973

"If you persist in doing the simple things in life perfectly, you'll have no trouble mastering difficult tasks, you'll be able to accomplish anything you want."

Noah Gregory could hear Lou repeating that phrase, it had become a non-stop sound loop in his mind. It was an adage Noah lived by and he considered it a gift, a gift which in all likelihood bore responsibility for his obsessive compulsive disorder. When you constantly strive for perfection, it's difficult to determine when you finally achieve it.

Lou, his adoptive father, was a lieutenant in the city fire department. He supervised a truck company out of station #3, and the men he supervised did the simple things to perfection. In Lou's world there was only one way to raise a ladder, only one way to get a victim onto the ladder, only one way to ventilate a roof, only one way to search a building for life or fire, and that was his way, an aggressive way, but a safe way.

On his days off, Lou installed roofs. Every nail perfectly driven into the tar lines of the shingles, every valley woven together like an expensive sweater, a chalk line dropped on every third tier of shingles to guarantee perfect symmetry, and every gutter flawlessly sloped to allow for the precise amount and speed of drainage. Every roof a work of art, every roof installed without a single, subsequent leak.

In the morning after waking up, Noah would make his bed. Perfect corners, the bedspread equally balanced from side to side. After showering, his teeth were brushed and flossed to perfection and there wasn't a drop of toothpaste left in the sink, nor a spot on the medicine cabinet mirror. His clothes were donned, the dress shirt tucked in without a wrinkle, a perfect knot in his tie, and his shoes were polished to mirror quality. If Lou was at the breakfast table after a night shift, Noah would hang onto his every word as he detailed the adventures of the night before – fires, large and small, car accidents, rescues, and the practical jokes firefighters delighted in playing on each other. Sometimes Lou would smell of smoke even after showering, and the constant exposure to heat and smoke was beginning to yellow his white hair.

Then it was off to St. Anthony's Academy. Noah would meet Alvin Bean on the way and they would journey up Elm Street and make a quick right onto Erie Avenue where the school was located.

Alvin didn't appreciate this route, but Noah always assured him it was the quickest, safest, and least traveled path to their school, and free of public school bullies.

"There they are again," mumbled Alvin, "those miserable bitches."

"Just ignore them," Noah advised, "they'll get theirs someday – we might not get to see it, but they'll get theirs someday."

Another pearl of wisdom from Lou, who had one for every occasion.

"When you're at bat, don't listen to the catcher or the crowd, the only way to shut them up is to ignore them and put the bat on the ball, a good solid smack, even if it's caught it sends the message you're not playing their game, they're playing yours."

"What if I strike out?"

"Then go down swinging, no sense in staring at strike three, can't get a hit if you don't swing the bat."

Lou had lots of baseball analogies, but it was hard to find one to fit the situation Alvin and Noah fell into most mornings on their way to ninth grade.

A group of four girls, all of whom attended ninth grade at St.

Anthony's, would gather on the corner of Jane and Elm Streets to re-adjust their plaid uniform skirts and pass a cigarette around. Out of sight of their mothers, they would hike their skirts up and smear some makeup on each other. More often than not, this act of rebellion was met with consternation, lectures, and a face scrubbing from one of the nuns.

"What are you looking at asshole – why don't you take a picture, it'll last longer."

Gretchen Moss, the ring leader, would deliver some rebukes to Noah and Alvin each day, but they would keep their heads down and plod on. There was no good way to argue with a girl at their age, and punching one in the face was definitely out of the question.

Gretchen, and some of her group, were dating older guys, juniors, seniors, a college freshman or two, and rumor had it Gretchen was quite cozy with a lay teacher at St. Anthony's.

"Hey fuck-face, why don't you take your pet retard and get the hell away from here."

Alvin had heard enough that morning, he was different and he accepted that, but he had reached a breaking point.

"Go to hell, you sluts," Alvin screamed at the top of his lungs, much to the amazement of the pack of hens on the corner.

No word at St. Anthony's could send a female into a frenzy more than the word slut. Not whore, not pig, but yet, Noah had heard Gretchen use those names on other girls who had the audacity to stand up to her. Hypocrisy. She had unabashedly mastered that trait.

And then it happened, four raging teenage girls were rushing Alvin and Noah, hell bent on some hair pulling, kicking and scratching, safe in the knowledge the duo wouldn't respond in kind.

Noah had to make a snap decision, was it more embarrassing to stand their ground and get their asses kicked, or more shameful to flat out run. Noah gave Alvin a stiff shove and the race was on. Noah could run like the wind, but Alvin was a wheezing mess, so Noah kept on Alvin's heels, pushing and encouraging him to keep moving.

"Now look what you've done Alvin, we're going to have to take a new way to school, all because you couldn't ignore those idiots."

"Sorry Noah, but I've taken too much shit, people just need to leave me alone."

They stood in the school courtyard, catching their breath, the Viking shield maidens had given up a block ago and secured their territory. Although Noah would chalk the day up to failure, he was to learn what a difference a year or two can make in adolescence.

At the end of their junior year, Gretchen took notice of Noah, forgetting the boy she once rejoiced in ridiculing. Noah thought it unusual when he caught Gretchen staring at him during math class, but he too felt an attraction instead of the animosity he once harbored for her.

By this time, the guys Gretchen and her friends had been dating were either drafted or lucky enough to get into college on deferments. The teacher she had been involved with was fired rather than arrested after numerous complaints from Gretchen's parents.

Noah became the new pair of shoes Gretchen and her posse would fight over – who would have the honor of indoctrinating him. Noah was confused when those girls started speaking to him, flirtatiously of course, and at first it went over his head. He'd never had a girl friend, he was awkward and shy around girls, but that was all about to change.

After a hair pulling match and a good old fashioned cat fight in the girls' bathroom, Gretchen had bested her group and now felt it necessary to put Noah between her paws.

In the summer that followed, Charlie Cossack and Dagger Lorow would host keg parties under some of the bridges spanning the river running through town. No one was sure how those two got their hands on the beer, but for a buck you could take part. They most often served as warm-ups before dances at the school or the YMCA. Teenage boys often need some liquid encouragement before they could muster the courage to ask a girl to slow dance. That was also the summer Charlie and Dagger started a new business, marijuana sales, and it was lucrative.

It was at such a party that Gretchen convinced Noah to sneak away from the crowd and smoke some pot with her. And, unfortunately, he liked it, and anything Noah liked he would overdo, another facet of his OCD. This was also his first experience with alcohol, and he enjoyed that even more.

Gretchen had created her Frankenstein monster, a willing one albeit, a monster she controlled with pot, booze, and sexual experimentation, not the torches used in the movies.

A year before, Noah had suffered a concussion during a baseball game. It was a frightful experience for him, memory loss, a sense of impending doom consumed him, along with a bizarre confusion which lasted for the better of two days. All this when he was mowed down by a base runner as he, the pitcher, covered first base perfectly, just as he had been coached. But the worst was yet to come. Two seizures, which he would never tell anyone about. He had no idea they were seizures, the nothingness and confusion convinced him he was going insane.

Over the years, he had heard his adoptive parents talk about Lou's sister who had been hospitalized with mental illness. The stories were horrific – shock therapy, straight-jackets, and mind numbing medications. Noah would rather die than experience that and the stigma it carried. Just ask Alvin Bean, his life had been a myriad of psychiatric treatments and derision. This led to Noah's coping rituals, which were easily accepted on a baseball field, but as they crept into everyday life, could be viewed as disturbing. Blessing yourself at bat, tapping your cleats with the bat a specific amount of times, inhaling and exhaling in a precise manner – all this to stave off another attack of the all consuming nothingness, and successful if done properly and in the correct order. So why couldn't these rituals be applied to everyday life, secretly of course. And therefore, he was compelled to do so.

Then came the intrusive thoughts, arriving like a runaway train. What if he was to just stand up in class and scream "Fuck" at the top of his lungs. What if he were to attack the baseball coach and choke him to death in front of the whole team. What if? And although he knew it was impossible to not think of something you didn't want to think of, these thoughts became haunting reminders of what might lie ahead for him.

But Gretchen, despite all her faults and hypocrisies, did come with a blessing. The booze and pot she fed Noah actually relieved his anxieties, they made him feel normal, and he relished feeling normal.

"You're acting kind of pissy today, what's up?"

Gretchen locked her arm around Noah's as they walked down the hall towards the auditorium.

"Just not looking forward to listening to another one of these guys go on and on about some bullshit I don't care about."

They were on the way to listen to another guest speaker in the auditorium. Most of these gentlemen were writing theses, or had written them, and were presenting to high school seniors for reaction and feed-back.

"You said the last one wasn't so bad, the guy who was listing stages of grief."

"I'm just kind of antsy, don't want to sit still for an hour or two."

"It's the booze, you're a different person when you mix pot and booze, you get angry."

Gretchen and Noah had polished off a pint of screwdriver and shared a joint in his car before classes began that day. She was right. When he mixed booze and marijuana he could get angry and it didn't take much of a trigger.

"I've got some valium I took from my mother, you want one, it might calm you down."

"Nah, if I'm lucky I'll fall asleep once this guy starts rambling on."

But sleep was not in the cards for Noah that day. The speaker was confrontational, sarcastic, and intelligent. His presentation centered upon accepting reality, being who you are and ignoring any dreams and aspirations that were in the slightest way unattainable. And his definition of unattainable was all encompassing. A depressing blanket of negativity soon fell over his audience.

"Let's face it," the speaker began, "all of you want to be rich and famous, but you know what, that's not going to happen for 99.9 per cent of you, and that's just a fact. Accepting that now will save you a lot of grief and disappointment in the future. Why strive for the unachievable, why suffer just to satisfy your ego or that of your parents'."

The speaker straightened his back, slid his glasses back upon his nose and stepped away from the podium. He began pointing at students and pronouncing what they would never be.

"You'll never be an Albert Einsten, no Thomas Edisons here, a Jonas Salk? I sincerely doubt it."

Noah was growing agitated. Who was this guy to tell anyone what they could never be.

"This son-of-a-bitch is starting to piss me off."

"Keep your voice down, you want detention again?"

Gretchen squeezed Noah's forearm, but he pulled her hand away.

"Okay, go ahead and get detention so you can sit there with your retarded little girl friend Diane. She's telling everyone you're in love with her."

Noah didn't like that word. Gretchen habitually used it to describe anyone she felt not in her social or intellectual class.

"Fuck off, she's not right, and you shouldn't be picking on her – you of all people – someone with the morals of a gerbil."

Some of the guys on the baseball team despised Gretchen so much they collected money in a coffee can and offered it to Noah if he would actually slap her around in front of them. Noah laughed it off, but he wondered what kind of person could garner so much disdain from so many.

"I'm outta here."

Noah stood and exited the auditorium. The other students watched as Gretchen ducked her head in embarrassment. The speaker paused for a moment before continuing.

It had been two months since Lou died, some form of lung cancer and probably job related. He insisted on coming home from the hospital to finish it out in his own surroundings. Joann, Noah's adoptive mother, agreed. She tried to be strong, but it was devastating for both her and Noah.

Firefighters would stop by once in a while, and Noah noticed one giving Lou a small bottle of pills. Noah wouldn't tell Joann, he knew what Lou was up to. Lou was going to exit on his own terms, he needed to end Joann's suffering.

"It's the simple things Noah, remember that."

Final words from a man who cast a very long shadow, even in death.

Noah could remember little about Lou other than that. As he

walked through the parking lot and to his car, Noah made a commitment to himself. With this afternoon's speaker in mind, he grumbled to himself and leaned against his car with both outstretched hands against the driver's side window.

"I will get to the big leagues like Lou always said I could, and I'll get there by doing things perfectly, the simple things, I will not fail Mr. Speaker, you motherfucker, I accept your challenge and someday I will return here and drag you back onto that stage for you to apologize for every dream you crushed today."

TO BE CONTINUED

ALBANY, NY
OCTOBER 1988

Lili-Che Faithful stood in the foyer of her apartment building checking her mail. And there it was. Another envelope addressed to her from a return address that according to the post office and the Albany Police Department, didn't exist.

Inside the envelope, as the habit had become, there was a stack of fresh twenty dollar bills. Fifty of them as usual. But this time there was something else. There appeared to be a letter tucked in as well. As she began to unfold it, her landlady, Mrs. Spicer, stepped from her first floor apartment and leaned against the wall of tenant mailboxes. She was holding a glass of beer in one hand, and as was the norm, a cigarette with an inch long ash hung from her mouth.

"Hattie, isn't it a little early for that?"

"I'm celebrating and you should be too – I sold this dump."

Lili quickly tucked the letter back into the envelope, hoping Mrs. Spicer hadn't noticed the stack of twenties.

"And just exactly why should I celebrate that, the rent will probably go up."

"That's just it," continued Mrs. Spicer, "we've been granted life time use of the place rent free, you and me."

"Rent free, why me?"

"I dunno, and I don't care. Some big guy showed up last week and offered me twice what the place is worth. Got the paper work today."

"Big guy?"

"Yeah, huge, nice dresser though, thought maybe you might know him. Had a funny accent."

"Doesn't sound like anyone I know. You better check this out, you know what they say about things that sound too good to be true."

"C'mon Lili, don't rain on our parade."

Lili could hear Mrs. Spicer's husband yelling from inside their apartment, but she couldn't make out what he was saying. Mrs. Spicer quickly turned and re-entered her apartment, beer in one hand, the cigarette in the other, and one knee high stocking rolled down to her ankle. Lili wondered if Mrs. Spicer ever wore anything but house coats. Her hair was habitually strung together with rollers and bobby pins and covered with a mesh sleep net.

As Lili approached the stairs she could hear Mrs. Spicer shouting at her husband.

"Make your own lunch Raymond, you lazy bastard."

An eccentric couple by far, but after the death of Lili's grandmother, they had showered Lili with concern and kindness, and an apartment for next to nothing.

Lili's heart raced as she climbed the steps to her apartment. What was the letter all about, some sort of explanation? Would her anonymous benefactor reveal himself, and just what was going on with Hattie selling this place. She could hear the TV blaring once she neared her apartment door. Her daughter Sofia was watching some Saturday morning shows at concert hall volume.

"Turn that down Sofia, you're being rude to the other people who live here."

Sofia obliged and sank back into the couch, her five year old frame obscured by a comforter.

The phone rang. Lili set the envelope down on the kitchen table and picked up the receiver. It was the girl who worked with her at the grocery store and at the club.

"Kate wants you back at the club tonight."

Kate ran the club and ruled the roost with a combination of frugality and motherly coercion, but she did have the safety of the girls foremost in her mind, and Lili respected that.

"Sorry, I'm done with that shit, a bunch of lechers pawing at me all night, it's just too much."

"Yeah, but the guys like you. They say you're exotic you know, you're different than the rest of us, and they like you being shy and all."

Lili looked at herself in the mirror above the phone. Yeah, she was exotic all right, people had always confused her ethnicity. Anything from Mexican to Iranian and all races in between. It happened so frequently she gave up correcting her questioners.

"Listen Sally, I appreciate you got me into the club, but I don't want to do it anymore. The tips are great, but by the time you tip the bartender and the bouncer, I might better be working extra shifts at the store."

"I've told you how to boost it Lili, just be a little friendlier, flirt some more, keep them drinking."

"I wish I could do that, but I just can't, gotta' go now, see you at the store on Monday."

"Have it your way then, but Kate would probably take you back if you change your mind, she likes you."

"Thanks, I'll see what happens."

Lili hung up and turned her attention to the letter. The money had been coming in like clockwork for the past three months. Twice a month, but never a note or letter enclosed. Never any sort of explanation. Maybe it was some geriatric pervert pissing away his life savings on her just because she allowed him to tuck a few bucks into her g-string.

She had tested the return address a few times by mailing empty envelopes to it, and they never came back. So, if it's not a real address, why don't the envelopes come back? The post office had done somewhat of an investigation, and the police paid the matter some halfhearted attention. She told them it was just a twenty arriving twice a month in an effort to cover all her bases. The money had been more than helpful, and there was no sense in ruining it if this was somehow an innocent act of kindness. She had decided to just shut up and let the whole thing run its course.

But maybe she should have been honest with them, it was two thousand dollars arriving a month, not forty. She rubbed the scar on her forehead as she sat at the kitchen table. She hoped playing it cool hadn't been a mistake.

"Not another mistake."

This could all blow up at any second. She unfolded the letter as if it could bite, and paid careful attention to its condition. Two pages, typewritten on heavy bond paper, and folded exactly as a business teacher had once instructed her to do.

Just then the television volume skyrocketed.

"Sofia, turn that down – do I have to get your hearing checked?"

BOMBS AWAY

ST. ANTHONY'S ACADEMY
1971

"What the hell is he up to now?"

Charlie Cossack and Dagger Lorow were seated across from each other in the cafeteria. Alvin Bean was sitting at a nearby table furiously opening Bazooka bubble gums, stacking the gum in one pile and the wrappers in another. This brand of chewing gum came with a miniature cartoon strip. Alvin was reading them in silence, his lips forming every unspoken word.

"He says he gets messages in the bubble gum, same old stuff – think he's just nervous because Larry's been picking on him, punching him in the arms a lot."

Charlie cupped a piece of bread and scooped spaghetti onto it with a fork, creating a soggy sandwich.

"It's the Dr. Otto thing again, pretty sad really."

Dagger didn't reply, his look of disgust said it all.

The Fat Larry incident, the trigger for Alvin's new bout of paranoia, occurred a few days earlier. Larry approached Alvin before the school doors opened that morning. There was the usual crowd and Larry thought it would be fun to harass Alvin for everyone's entertainment. But the entertainment backfired.

"Hey Bean, does your mother feed you ugly pills?"

"Does your mother feed you basketballs?"

Alvin's reply was delivered sharply, without hesitation, and Larry was furious at being one-upped.

"We're next you know," Charlie stuffed his creation into his mouth, "after Larry beats the hell out of Alvin, he's coming for us, he knows we're on probation, we can't do shit to him."

"We'll see about that."

Dagger watched Charlie pile spaghetti onto another piece of bread and decided to do the same.

But Charlie was correct, they were both on probation, and Dagger had spent the end of the last school year at a youth correctional facility known as Industry. Since it was Charlie's first offense, he was allowed to remain home, suspended from school for one week, and now supervised by a court ordered probation officer.

As head strong and criminally inclined as Dagger had been, once he returned from Industry, he felt totally unbound. His mind churned with a newfound insight into societal behavior. Take from the takers, never stop taking, not for an instant, and punish anyone who gets in the way.

He shaped his own philosophy while at the correctional facility, and in the process redefined his concept of right and wrong. He paid close attention to the hierarchies there, and especially to the personalities involved. Guards and detainees. It wasn't about being the leader, it was about knowing who was next in line – that was the ever present danger his colleagues didn't understand. That was the key to the puzzle, the cornerstone of his dogma.

While there, Dagger busied himself with the machine shop, and became knowledgeable with every tool in the facility. What was the tool intended to be used for, could it cut, could it pry, did it have any other potential applications. Anything mechanical had to be assembled, and therefore, anything assembled could be disassembled. Some tools had multiple applications. That interested Dagger the most. Handles of pliers could be sharpened, to function as awls, punches or screw drivers, adding a pipe to a wrench handle could increase its torque. Dagger loved the simplicity of it all. He would put this knowledge to good use in the future.

And though it is laughable now, he even attended a course on locksmithing – everything from opening automobile doors to after-market dead bolt installations. Really, Dagger thought, are these people for real.

With this newly acquired knowledge, he could open most locked doors with a pair of water pump pliers and a hefty screw driver, and he could do it in short order with little damage, and he could replace the lock cylinder when done. Most of his burglaries were undetectable. Sometimes he would enter, find a key, a spare most often kept in the manager's desk, replace the lock and return the key after having it duplicated. On return visits, Dagger and Charlie greedily helped themselves to whatever they could use or sell. There wasn't a beer or liquor supplier in the city that Dagger and Charlie didn't have a key to. Dagger often wondered why someone at these establishments didn't question their dwindling inventories, but then again, they probably thought it was the usual employee thievery, up and down the ladder.

Fat Larry, as he was referred to when out of earshot, had been terrorizing the sophomore class with his threats and bullying. Sooner or later, everyone was in the barrel, it was their turn to be embarrassed and harassed. Larry was a tough kid, he knew how to fight and he enjoyed it, but he seemed to enjoy taunting the defenseless even more.

"Hey jail bird, you think you're pretty tough, huh?"

Larry had issued that threat to Dagger after delivering a swift punch to Dagger's upper arm, in hopes of leaving a bruise, his calling card. Dagger didn't respond, he walked effortlessly down the hall much to Larry's dismay.

But Dagger would have to wait, Alvin Bean was now in the crosshairs. How Larry loved to gather a crowd around Alvin as he debased him. Alvin would respond with some foolish threat of retaliation, which delighted the crowd even more. And then the day came when Alvin was challenged to meet Larry after school in the alley behind Obeida's pool hall. Alvin had dodged him for a week, but today was to be the day.

In the interim, Charlie and Dagger had been busy with their own form of pre-emptive retaliation. In the dead of night, Charlie boosted Dagger up a telephone pole in the alley behind Larry's house. Voila, Larry's family had just lost television and phone service. And the next night, a brick crashed through the window of Larry's grandmother's house, and then, the following evening, some acid was applied to the top of the convertible Larry's father so loved. All of this done to encourage a pause in Larry's campaign of brutality. But to no avail.

"Could he really be this stupid?"

Charlie looked at Dagger after the acid incident, after all, the acid was reported stolen from the high school chemistry lab a day earlier and multiple students were questioned.

"Maybe, but I'm not going to be at Alvin's beating today, got a dentist's appointment – guess I'm lucky, hate to see that fat bastard abuse him anymore."

"We've done everything but burn his house down and he still doesn't think he's made some enemies."

Charlie was dumbfounded.

The afternoon of the beating arrived. Alvin occupied himself in study hall by making an effigy of Larry with a chalkboard eraser. He attached a drawing of Larry to the eraser with masking tape and drove push pins into it, hoping it would disable Larry, making him unable to attend the scheduled alley fight. There would, however, be no hope of escaping the violence, supernatural effigy or not. Alvin was pushed towards the alley by a group of students after dismissal. And there stood Larry. He removed his glasses, his one eye, the lazy eye, was slightly askew, there was a small scar next to it, an ominous grin was plastered across his face. Unbridled eagerness in this next act of barbarism was coursing through his frame, how he enjoyed the superiority cruelty gave him.

Charlie was purposely late to the event. He kept his distance, for sometimes, after Larry finished destroying someone verbally and physically, he scanned the crowd for a new victim. Charlie's probation would be up in a month, he didn't need anything to impede that.

When Charlie arrived, Larry was pushing Alvin into the observers, one shove after another, goading him to make the first move, throw the first punch. Hands from the crowd pushed Alvin back into the center of the newly formed circle. Alvin steadied himself into the stance of a martial artist and the crowd howled along with Larry.

And then came a dull thud, followed by broken glass and the sound of gravel spilling into the alley, a sound similar to that of a hard rain. Larry was rendered motionless on the pavement. The crowd scattered, only Charlie and Alvin remained.

"You better get outta' here."

Charlie gave Alvin a push before he turned and ran in the other direction.

Charlie stopped running as he turned down East Main Street. Better walk the rest of the way, no sense in attracting any attention to himself. It was all beginning to make sense. Every day after school, Dagger would grab a pocket full of gravel from Steinbrenner's driveway and toss the stones, one at a time, into the road as they walked home. And their last act of retribution was particularly vile but pertinent to today's event. Larry's family still had a milk box on their front porch. Every morning the milkman would replace the empties with full ones. How angry and surprised the milkman would be to find an empty bottle now filled with urine. Dagger must have taken an extra bottle and filled it with driveway stone. No coincidence that Dagger left school earlier in the afternoon for a supposed dentist's appointment.

It would have been a simple task to get onto the fire escape from the dumpster beneath it, and then three floors up. It would have been difficult to carry the milk bottle up the steep metal ladder leading to the roof from the last escape platform – tough but doable. An easy escape could be made a few buildings away during the ensuing confusion. The alley was littered with rusty, rickety fire escapes from one end to the other. Dropping the milk bottle was an act of precision though, and it could have been fatal, or he could have hit Alvin. But that was Dagger, he took chances when he felt in control of the circumstances.

Larry showed up at school a few days after he was released from the hospital wearing some sort of back brace and neck collar. He looked ridiculous, and no one was the wiser as to the identity of the assassin.

On the day of Larry's return, Alvin entered the cafeteria and set his tray down next to Charlie's. His demeanor was jovial, there was an obvious sense of satisfaction and relief about him. He stared at Larry who was still going through the lunch line. Larry wouldn't make eye contact with him.

"That voodoo doll must have done it alright, just like Dr. Otto said it would, doesn't look like he'll be bothering me for a while."

"You must have some sort of magic Alvin."

Dagger patted Alvin on the back and gave a quick wink to Charlie.

MIDNIGHT MISERY

THE BOTTOMS UP CLUB
UTICA, NY
ONE WEEK AFTER ALVIN BEAN'S IMMOLATION

Hannigan Butler met Wendy Montana in the Champagne Room after paying for a private dance. The room, clad in mirrors, was dimly lit. The overhead black light exposed every speck of lint, dandruff, and dust.

Wendy, clad only in a g-string, eased the door shut as she made her entrance.

"The g-string comes off for another twenty bucks, and if you get stupid, the bouncer will be in here in seconds."

"I won't get stupid, promise."

Hannigan handed her a fifty dollar bill, she looked surprised, tucked the bill into her garter and dropped the g-string.

"Listen, this isn't really about a dance…"

"Are you a fucking cop – I'm not a whore."

"No, I'm not a cop, and I'm not here to entrap you, I'm a private investigator, I'd like to ask you about the fire at the nursing facility."

"I don't know a fucking thing about that fire, I already told the cops why I was there, and that was a day before that guy burned up."

That much was true. But, Wendy had visited the facility in order to kill a patient, a patient who she knew from adolescence, an adolescence fraught with fear and abuse. And that patient was not the man who burned, that man was someone she believed needed to be sent to hell. She told the police none of that.

Karl McCarthy, better known as Hoss, had been moved to the nursing home a few months prior to Wendy's visit. Wendy met Hoss's brother one evening at the club. The brother had come to Utica to visit Hoss and was telling Wendy of his circumstances during some drinks and private dances.

As the conversation progressed, Wendy was able to piece together who this man's brother actually was. As soon as he referred to him as Hoss, the flashback struck like a lightning bolt.

This man's brother was the sadistic bastard who made her life a living hell when she was admitted to Juvenile Psych after a botched suicide attempt. His visits, precisely at midnight, could not be forgiven. The nightmarish visions of this large man with a crew cut – a Polaroid camera in his hand, quietly unlocking her room door, could not be forgotten. The devilish smile upon his face as he put his finger to his lips, warning her to be silent, screamed for vengeance. Righteous vengeance.

And then there was the event that ended Hoss's reign of torture. Wendy heard staff at the Psych Center talk among themselves about Hoss's condition. Brain dead was the term used. Good, thought Wendy, but that was too nice for him after what he had put her through. And no one had questioned her about the camera or why he was found unconscious outside her room.

The kid she saw at the door the night Hoss hit the floor, that scared kid called Beanie, she never told a soul what she saw that night. God bless that kid, and to hell with those adults who knew what that son-of-a-bitch was up to and did nothing. But now it would be Wendy's chance to pay Hoss a visit and she promised herself it would be ugly, it would be cruel, but it would be justified.

"I know what you told the cops, and I don't blame you a bit."

"That guy was a fucking pervert, that's why I called him out, and the cops agreed with me."

Wendy slid her g-string back on and offered the fifty back to Hannigan.

"I don't want it, honest," Hannigan remained seated, "I'm not accusing you of anything, I just would like to know if you saw anything out of the ordinary."

Hannigan paid careful attention to the tattoos running down Wendy's arms, from her shoulders to her wrists. They quite possibly hid injection sites, she appeared high as well as angry, but the tattoo on the small of her back, the proverbial tramp stamp, was unusual. An ornate clock, the type that could be found atop a fireplace mantel, the clock hands positioned at twelve o'clock, and on each side of the clock, a cherub, kneeling and weeping.

Wendy had visited Hoss's room the day before the fire. She gave the facility receptionist a fake name and told the woman she was there to visit Hoss, her uncle. She assured the receptionist she had no intention of getting a glimpse of the bird a small crowd of people had assembled outside to see. She was not there to sneak a peek from the inside. She was not a bird watcher or a believer in miracles, that day she was an assassin. Besides, a white cardinal, she thought, big deal, how could that relate to hope or religion.

Wendy carried a large hand bag that day. She told the receptionist she planned on leaving some family pictures in Hoss's room. But the bag contained no family photos, just a Polaroid camera, a folded makeshift sign, and a syringe full of antifreeze.

She pulled up a chair next to Hoss's bed and took a careful look at him and his surroundings. He was gaunt and pale, garbed only in a hospital gown and covered to the waist by a sheet. A catheter bag hung on the bed frame and a tube from an elevated plastic bag ran into his abdomen. He was bald, his mouth agape with spittle running down one side. His hands were slid into what appeared to be mittens, larger versions of what babies wear to keep from scratching themselves, a blank, incoherent stare filled his bloodshot eyes.

Wendy drew the curtain separating Hoss from the neighboring

patient. The patient was sound asleep, a snore whistled from his nose, interrupted occasionally by a weak cough. A nurse passed by in the hallway, on her way to answer a buzzer from another room. There would never be a better time to put an end to Hoss than now. Wendy felt her heart pounding, a slight nausea overtook her stomach. The time was now she thought. It had to be done now and done quickly.

Wendy looked into her bag at the syringe, but, could his death be any worse than what he was experiencing now. After all, she thought, he was at present serving a life sentence, and if he were to die, if there is a hell, he would spend eternity there, but if there was no hell, she would be doing him a favor, and if there is only a heaven, she could not bear believing he could possibly arrive there.

No, death would not visit Upstate Skilled Nursing that day, but revenge would. She took the sign from her bag and fastened it around his neck with the attached string. After unfolding the camera, she stood at the foot of the bed and took a picture of what she had done. She shook the photo in one hand and watched it develop as she set the camera down on the nearby nightstand.

She was going to mail the photo to Hoss's brother, or maybe to the hospital where Hoss committed his crimes and fell under no scrutiny for them. Yes, that would be a better revenge than freeing him from this miserable existence. She convinced herself this was not mercy, this was retribution.

"So that's all you did to that puke, hang a sign around his neck?"

"The cops told you that too, huh?"

Wendy was snapped back to the present by Hannigan's question.

"Yeah, that's all I did, hung a sign on him calling him out as a child molester, for all to see – and you know what, I bet some of his caregivers don't care too much for him anymore, what do you think."

Hannigan nodded in agreement and stood. He pulled a business card from his pocket and presented it to Wendy.

"There's a phone number on the back, it's the hotel where I'm at, if you remember anything about that day – anything relating to the fire or Alvin Bean, give me a call."

That was the truly odd factor about her failed attempt at murder, could this Alvin Bean be the kid from Juvenile Psych, could he be Beanie, was this his punishment for bringing Hoss down that night, and why should he be punished for ending her misery, that was the paradox reeling about Wendy's mind.

"Never knew any Alvin Bean, and I can't think of anything strange about that day other than what I did – and I'll never be sorry for it."

"I understand, believe me, maybe sometime we could talk outside of this place."

"Maybe."

Wendy accepted the card and folded it into the fifty dollar bill in her hand. There was something disturbing about this guy she couldn't put her finger on, but she knew the next time she was high or drunk, depressed or manic, she would give that number a call.

MR. COSSACK IS AT THE DOOR

BINGHAMTON, NY
1989

Teddy Pulver had been advocating for the disabled for more than a decade. After his accident and the soul crushing depression it brought with it, Teddy decided to make the best of what was left of his life. No more cynicism, no more anger, he would channel those emotions into a positive drive – he would help others suffering from the realization they would never walk again. He knew all too well the ravages of hopelessness and despair.

He lobbied tirelessly for the handicapped. He took on politicians, health insurance companies, and fought for the accommodations, accessibility, and respect that the handicapped deserved. And he was successful. Laws were passed, insurance claims were reviewed and properly compensated – his lobby had become a powerful influencer and a voting bloc to be reckoned with.

On a personal level, Teddy married, he owned a home, and his name was being floated for a shot at a state wide office. He was courted by donors, each with their own agenda, but he promised himself to stay true to what had rescued him from his darkest days – a commitment to a just cause, a purpose he would not abandon.

Charlie Cossack, a potential donor, had requested a meeting with Teddy to discuss some proposed legislation and possible support for Teddy's political ambitions. Mr. Cossack requested to meet at Teddy's home. He wanted to keep the meeting low key. No one else needed to know until he made the decision to back Teddy.

Teddy agreed. Mr. Cossack arrived in a black limousine, parked conspicuously in front of Teddy's ranch style home in the Binghamton suburbs. Teddy watched from his office window as two very large men exited the vehicle along with Mr. Cossack. One of the men walked with Cossack to the front door, the other made his way to the rear of the house.

"Teddy, why is there a guy standing by our back door?"

Elizabeth, Teddy's wife, shouted her question to Teddy from the kitchen where she had spotted the giant in the back yard.

"It's alright Liz, he's with the guy I'm meeting with, will you please let him in, he's out front."

Elizabeth greeted Cossack at the front door and showed him into Teddy's office. Cossack's associate remained outside, gazing up and down the street. Teddy thought the scene was a little too cloak and dagger to be taken seriously, but it did lighten up a boring Saturday afternoon in the suburbs.

Elizabeth made her way back to the kitchen after closing the office door behind her. Cossack carried a briefcase which he placed on the floor next to the chair he seated himself in. He smiled and made unflinching eye contact with Teddy. The type of eye contact which can easily be interpreted as anger, the type of anger which most often foreshadows violence.

"Mr. Pulver, we've met a couple times, but I'm sure you don't remember me, they weren't pleasant occasions, for me anyway."

"I don't recall ever meeting you Mr. Cossack, you have me at a disadvantage here."

Teddy was uncomfortable with Cossack's tone.

"You can call me Charlie, or better yet, dumb polack, does that ring a bell?"

Teddy was about to move his motorized wheel chair from behind the desk he was seated at to show Cossack to the door, but Cossack quickly opened the briefcase and pointed a pistol at Teddy.

"Stay put Teddy, I want to remind you of who I am and why I'm here."

"Please, don't hurt my wife, do what you want to me, but don't hurt my wife."

"Rest assured, we won't touch a hair on her head, just keep your voice down and we can get on with this."

Cossack laid the pistol on top of the briefcase now positioned on his lap.

"The first time we met I was only ten or eleven years old, you were older though, there was a kickball game behind St. Anthony's in Utica, remember that?"

"I used to visit my aunt there, but I don't remember you."

"I'm that kid you kicked the shit out of, you knocked out a tooth, ruptured my ear drum, and broke my nose, and you really liked doing it, remember that?"

Cossack's eyes remained focused on Teddy, he spoke slightly above a whisper, but it was obvious he was agitated.

"But you do remember Teddy, don't you, you called me a dumb polack, remember that, I sure the fuck do, but I could never figure out how you knew my family changed their name, now I'm guessing your aunt must have told you."

"I was a mean kid, an asshole of a kid, I'll admit that, and I probably did rough you up."

"It was more than a simple roughing up, you pinned me to the ground and punched the hell out of me, you were bigger, you were older, you had the advantage and you enjoyed it, didn't you?"

"Unfortunately, I probably did, is that what this is all about, a childhood fight, some sort of fucked up revenge twenty-some years later, look at me, I've been punished enough, don't you think."

"We met again in college, you were kicking a soccer ball around in the lounge and you kicked it right into the side of my head, and you thought it was hilarious, you and your friends."

Elizabeth tapped at the door.

"Would Mr. Cossack like some coffee?"

Cossack pointed the pistol at Teddy and shook his head.

"No thanks Liz, we're finishing up."

"If I remember, you had done two years in the service before college, I was only there for a semester, but you strutted around the dorm like the top dog – big mistake kicking that soccer ball into my face."

"I'm sorry I did that, I can't take it back now, but you must want something, what is it you want, you want to kill me?"

"I want you to thank me."

"Thank you for what, I have no idea what you're talking about."

"Thank me for giving you the gift of humility."

Cossack repositioned himself in the chair and leaned over. He wanted to emphasize what he was about to say.

"You didn't fall down those stairs at the dorm, sure, you were drunk, but I kicked you down those stairs from behind, I even whispered into your ear after I did it, remember what I said – you must remember that, don't you?"

"You called me a piece of shit and said you weren't Polish, I thought it was all just a dream, a hallucination, it didn't make any sense, but now you want me to thank you for that?"

"If you want the money that's in this briefcase you will – I rescued you from a life of arrogance and selfishness, you are the person you are now because of me, I am the only reason. There's enough cash here to make a real difference in a lot of people's lives – if you want it, thank me."

"What if I don't?"

"Then I leave, no harm, no foul, and I wouldn't bother calling the police, the Watch Commander and I had breakfast together this morning, he accepted a briefcase very similar to this one."

"This is just too unbelievable to be true."

A tear ran down Teddy's cheek, but he was unable to raise his arm to wipe it off. Cossack stood and walked towards him. Teddy feared death might be approaching, but Cossack pulled a handkerchief from his suit coat pocket and dabbed the tear away.

"I don't know why I'm telling you this Teddy, but lately I've been corresponding with a very dear friend, and she's been urging me to atone, to apologize for some of the things I've done, but I'm really struggling with forgiving you, my truth is I don't regret paralyzing you, I can't apologize, and that will not bode well for me, I know."

Cossack pocketed the handkerchief, tucked the pistol into his waist band, and set the briefcase on Teddy's desk. He slowly moved towards the door before turning to look again at the sobbing Teddy Pulver.

"Keep the money and do something good with it, you won't see me again."

"Thank you Mr. Cossack."

THE TOMATO SOUP INCIDENT

THE A&P MARKET
UTICA, NY
1960

Charlie Cossack sat at his office desk, re-reading the letters Lili-Che Faithful had sent him. They had been corresponding for nearly six months with an unfortunate, but necessary lag time between letters. Charlie wanted to keep their relationship a secret for now, so he created a convoluted path for their communications to travel.

Upon his urging, Lili rented a box at the post office where his letters were hand delivered, minus postage, along with return addresses that didn't exist. Her return messages were intercepted by his operatives in Albany with some assistance from corrupt post office employees and police officers. This entire operation was under the influence of Charlie's body man, Gennady.

Gennady briefed his posse of scammers, extortionists, and thieves as to their new priorities. The letters come first. Fake insurance claims come second, stealing catalytic converters and luxury vehicles comes third, while marketing bootleg cigarettes would be a distant fourth. The letters were to keep moving at all cost, and those who transited them were to keep their mouths shut as to this enterprise. Lili had no idea who Charlie actually was, the name he assigned to his letters was admittedly an alias, and at present, he warned her, it was much too dangerous for him to reveal his identity.

A rare form of trauma induced amnesia had wiped the real Charlie Cossack from her mind, and that, Charlie thought, was a gift from God. Charlie wanted to keep his employer completely unaware of Lili's existence. So now, Charlie sat at his desk at the Bar & Grill in Utica, typing another epistle to the woman he obsessed upon, while at the same time focusing on the demise of his employer, all to be done for Lili's safety and their eventual reunion. He would not allow her to become a bargaining chip. That was his paramount concern. He had given her snippets of the man he had become through their letters to one another, but he worried she would not accept all he had done. There was also the possibility she was only continuing their correspondence because of the money and gifts he, her mysterious benefactor, sent, along with the cryptic clues as to his identity. He tried hard not to think of that possibility. Charlie's missives, originally an attempt at seduction, now evolved into self-reflection. Could he be the man Lili-Che deserves.

Somehow, Charlie thought, he had managed to sacrifice most of his conscience before the age of fourteen. As a young man he didn't deliberately seek to harm anyone out of superiority or malice, but God help them if they got in the way. His ancestors, the warriors, the marauders, the anarchists, and even the poets would be proud. The cold hearted vengeance he exacted on enemies and rivals would delight and inspire them. As to those ancestors, Charlie believed genetics played an important part in his development, along with an occasional nudge from a childhood friend named Dagger Lorow, who never lacked for inciting thievery or violence. It was at times, both casual and terrifying, but never boring.

As a child, Charlie was surrounded by strong women. His mother and aunts were confrontational, unyielding, outspoken, and never apologetic. They stood their ground, win or lose, they didn't back down. Their attitudes, much like Charlie's could be attributed to a blend of genetics and familial environment. True, he thought, the environment he was raised in could predispose sociopathic character traits in male offspring who carried just the right mix of genetics. History blamed dominant mothers and violently abusive fathers as the factors shaping Hitler and Stalin, but they were also psychopaths, and at present, Charlie managed to walk that tightrope.

Whenever Charlie preoccupied himself with the factors that affected his beliefs and attitudes, and fueled his insatiable appetite for revenge, he would dwell on one incident involving his mother, perhaps the single most personality shaping incident of his life, which occurred at the local A&P market, not at a riot or in a war zone. This incident was tattooed upon his psyche with equal parts of admiration and bewilderment.

While grocery shopping with his mother, at the age of four or five, Charlie was knocked out the cart he was standing in by a rude and hurried shopper. He was standing in the cart, eyeballing the store and customers. The store itself was on the smaller size for what it contained. The aisles were packed and narrowed because of that. This stood out to Charlie, even at his young age. Customers had to carefully maneuver their carts around one another, and there was the occasional banging of cart on cart, and the interlocking of wheels. The wheels on the cart Charlie rode in were squeaky and would sometimes lock up when the cart cornered. Charlie was told to hang on when a turn approached.

There was a woman rushing down the aisle perpendicular to the cart Charlie's mother was pushing. Without warning, the woman swung her cart into the aisle where Charlie was. In an instant she slammed into Charlie and unseated him. He fell face first onto the concrete floor and landed with a crisp smack. He could feel his throbbing forehead swell as he broke into tears. He gasped for breath out of fear and pain. The woman was unimpressed, and mumbled a halfhearted apology as she sped by.

In one fluid motion, Charlie's mother grabbed the woman's coat with one hand and began swinging a can of Campbell's tomato soup into the back of her head with the other hand. The woman tried to wrestle the soup can from Charlie's mother, but she was unsuccessful. His mother swung, and swung, until the woman lay on the floor. The woman's appearance resembled that of a dead spider. Blood streamed from her nose and mouth. There were deep gashes along her forehead and eyebrows as well. Blood pooled along the back of her head where the initial blows struck.

The store manager appeared, but maintained a clear distance from Charlie's mother and her soup can turned weapon. As he opened his mouth to speak, Charlie's mother interrupted.

"Get the fuck away from me."

He obeyed, and mother and child abandoned their shopping cart and rushed from the store. Charlie was held tight by his mother who tossed the bloodied can of tomato soup over her shoulder.

The police arrived later that day and took Charlie's mother into custody. He felt it so unjust that he was slammed to the ground, perhaps intentionally, but definitely recklessly, and his mother was arrested for defending him.

His mother returned home later that day in the custody of his father. There were a couple court appearances and a fine before the matter was dropped. The event itself was never discussed again in Charlie's house.

In hindsight, Charlie knew the incident was due to pure carelessness, not malice, but his visceral feeling about the incident would never change. Protect your own, and what you love at all costs, defend in the moment, attack in the moment, and regret nothing. Sympathy and empathy are just words when rage responds – use that rage, channel that rage, send a message of strength in the midst of a crisis through that rage. That is all that matters. All that ever will.

But instantaneous revenge, though thoroughly gratifying, is sometimes impossible. There are some occasions which call for a unrepentant malevolence which can only be achieved through patience and planning, duplicity and stealth, and Charlie was prepared to spend a lifetime cultivating those attributes. Lili-Che Faithful would be his once again.

FLAMING ARROW

THE AMERICAN EMBASSY
WEST BERLIN
1991

Noah Gregory was led down the hallway of the American Embassy, handcuffed and wearing leg chains. He was directed into an interrogation room by a United States Marine and instructed to be seated at an interview table. His handcuffs were locked to a hasp on that table. The metal folding chair he sat on was cold and uncomfortable.

On the table, to one side, was a reel to reel tape recorder and what appeared to be a small stack of passports. The blinds were drawn on the window behind him and directly above was a fluorescent light fixture, one of the tubes blinked every few seconds.

Noah had been hospitalized at a U.S. military base since the prisoner exchange. He was positive the cancer would take him before the swap. His prison sentence in Belarus had been riddled with worsening sickness and malnutrition which he attributed to the cancer. Now though, he felt stronger, he had an appetite, and the fever had broken. He turned to see himself in the wall mounted mirror, a mirror which shielded his interrogators from him. His face was pale and scarred from his cheeks to his temples. His dark hair was peppered with gray and uncombed. He had been given a nylon track suit to wear for today's interview, it was too large, it was apparent he had lost weight during his imprisonment and hospitalization. His sense of time had become distorted due to the sickness and isolation. How long he thought, weeks, years, months, he was unsure, it was all a jumble.

This cancer is a funny disease he thought, you prepare to die every day, some days you want to and some days you don't, and if that isn't punishment enough, I'm probably headed to another prison once they get done with me today. At least, maybe then, in an American prison, I'll be able to make my final peace with my daughter and mother, even if it's through a glass divider.

The door opened and in walked Noah's interrogator. Noah heard the door click shut and lock. The interrogator brought with him a file and an ashtray. He seated himself on the opposite side of the table, lit a cigarette and flipped a switch on the tape recorder. Noah watched the reels begin to turn before observing the man seated across from him.

"Mr. Gregory, could you tell me your full name, date of birth, and if you remember, your social security number."

"You know who you look like," asked Noah, "you look just like George Foreman, are you here to punch the hell out of me to get a confession?"

Noah smiled, the interrogator did not. Not much of a sense of humor with this guy.

"No one's going to punch you today Mr. Gregory, we just need to clear up some details about the passports you have used and the people you traveled with, and yes, I have heard that before, so, let's just get on with this."

"Ask away, I've got nothing to lose, I've got terminal cancer you know, so I could give a shit about anything, ask away."

After Noah's diagnosis, he plotted to take care of his daughter Marta and his mother Joanne. The death benefit from the fire department would be eaten up in a few years, and any other benefits would be a mere pittance. His alcoholism had worsened along with the stress, but it brought with it a new attitude, a "fuck it" attitude. The guys at the station would refer to it as that when they got closer to their retirement date. This new attitude helped Noah accept Charlie Cossack's offer.

"You don't have cancer Mr. Gregory, you've been hospitalized here for two weeks with a small pox infection you picked up in prison along with a dose of tuberculosis, you're lucky to be alive, but you don't have cancer, and to be honest with you, you would've died there if we didn't have reason to believe you were Charles Cossack."

"What the hell are you talking about, I was told I had terminal stage prostate cancer?"

"They've run every test in the book on you Mr. Gregory, and you don't have prostate cancer."

The interrogator opened his file and slid hospital discharge papers across the table for Noah to review. Noah read the diagnosis, and the test results. Cancer of any type was not listed, just the small pox and tuberculosis.

"Well, let's get on with this Mr. Gregory, I'm going to ask you a series of questions I already know the answers to, and if you answer truthfully, we'll figure out what to do with you next."

Noah shook his head in agreement.

"Have you ever traveled under the names of Charles Cossack, Gabriel Golovkin, Alvin Bean, or Alan Lorow?"

The interrogator opened each passport stacked on the table as he asked his question.

"Yes to each one of those."

"Can you state for the purpose of this interview that you are not Charles Cossack."

"I'm not him, but I know him."

"How do you know Charles Cossack, and why were you using the passports I showed you?"

"We grew up together, I asked him to do me a favor when I found out I had cancer, I wanted to get a life insurance policy to take care of my daughter, he was into that sort of stuff."

"We're well aware of the rampant insurance fraud committed by Mr. Cossack, but why did you assume his identity and aliases?"

"Listen, my pension would've been shit and I couldn't get a policy because of the cancer, Charlie said if I made an overseas trip as him, he'd take care of my mother and daughter, so I did it."

"What about the woman and her brothers you traveled with, what's their story?"

A reference to Mary Regis O'Malley and her brothers Sean and Owen. The O'Malleys had been assigned to travel with Noah, partly as security and partly to reinforce the concept he was actually Charles Cossack. In return, the O'Malleys were promised a veritable arsenal of weapons including shoulder launch missiles. Their father and his confederates were imprisoned in Northern Ireland and labeled as terrorists by the British government. The weapons were to be used in an all out assault on the prison in an effort to free their comrades. It sounded like a suicide mission to Noah, but he counted on being dead long before that could happen.

"Irish lunatics, but I hit it off with Mary Regis, there was just something about her. You know, she could've been a concert violinist."

Noah tried to lean back in his chair, but being fastened to the table hampered his movement. Despite his glib answers, Noah worried Mary Regis had been imprisoned, or worse yet killed, but he had worked hard to convince himself she escaped from the hotel where he was taken prisoner.

"You might be interested in learning your Irish cohorts have recently been released in a prisoner exchange between the United Kingdom and Somalia. The Brits got a diplomat back, and the Somalis got your pals. We're still trying to figure that one out, but it stinks of your friend Cossack."

That was a relief, after the gunfire in the hotel lobby in Kyiv,

Noah was auctioned off to Belarus, now he knew for sure Mary Regis was alive. He hoped her imprisonment hadn't been as harsh as his and that her deal included a safe asylum. He felt a sense of relief with those thoughts.

"How about unlocking me from the table, I'm as weak as a kitten, I'm no threat, and I'm not believing that stuff about not having cancer."

The interrogator complied and offered Noah a cigarette after doing so.

"No thanks, they cause cancer you know."

Noah waited for a laugh from the interrogator, but there wasn't one.

"Let's talk some more about the O'Malleys, how did you meet them and why."

"Charlie put me in her custody after the fire in Lackawanna, if you know everything like you said, you probably know that warehouse fire was set and inside were some guys that came hunting for him."

"Did you participate in those murders?"

"Gave him some advice on how to do the fire, didn't know there would be people inside. It was an old steel plant used to store boats and RVs. Those boats are made of fiberglass, and that's as bad as gasoline when it comes to feeding a fire. I was nowhere near the building when it went up."

"So you remained outside when they lit the fire, how's it feel to be a party to arson after being a firefighter and an arson investigator?"

"Didn't feel good, especially with the people inside and all. I waited uphill, in a small field in the industrial park. When they returned in the limo, the big guy was stinking of gasoline. He took a bow and arrow out of the trunk and wrapped something around an arrow and launched it towards the building after he lit it."

"A flaming arrow – that sounds ridiculous."

"No shit, it went through a busted out window and the place went up quick, you must've seen the pictures, it looked like Hiroshima when the bomb hit."

"Yes, I saw it on the news, luckily for you, no responders were hurt."

"That was the whole idea, have it burning so hot and big, it would be a surround and drown."

"Well, Mr. Gregory, in addition to three dead Serbians, we found identification belonging to Charles Cossack on one of them, so why did he have you roaming around the globe with terrorists if he wanted us to believe he died in the fire?"

"He knew the body in there wouldn't match his identification, so he knew after a while you'd be on to that, so he sent me off to create a wild goose chase to pull you away from where he was going."

"And, do you, or the O'Malleys, know where he escaped to?"

"Not a clue, listen, I had no idea how much stuff he was into, that wasn't the guy I knew when we were kids, never expected anything like that out of him."

"Let me educate you on some of the crimes Mr. Cossack is suspected of – he sold landmines to warring factions in Angola and Sri Lanka, he supplied child soldiers in Africa with assault rifles and methamphetamine, he more than likely is responsible for the murder of his boss in Toronto, and he is wanted in the Philippines in regards to a political assassination, all of that in addition to the conflagration in Lackawanna, New York."

Noah shrugged his shoulders in disbelief.

"One last question Noah, why you?"

"We were always pretty similar in looks, people would mistake us for brothers, but I was adopted. There was a school nurse who used to call us 'other mother brothers.' Guess I fit the bill – that's what he wanted in exchange for helping me – must've thought I had nothing to lose, and he was right."

"Do you think he lived up to his part of the bargain?"

"I kinda' think he probably did somehow, that's the one thing about him, even as a kid, when he said he was going to do something, he did it."

"You might be correct, your daughter and mother were last seen boarding a private jet in Florida. That was well over a year ago."

Noah smiled and thought to himself, that son-of-a-bitch did it, he set them up like he said he would. Facing death just got easier, but if what this guy says is true, I might be serving the rest of a long life in prison.

"So how does witness protection work, would it work for me?"

"It's not going to work for you Noah. Do you have any idea who I am, I didn't tell you my name."

The interrogator opened the file again and handed Noah a newspaper clipping and switched off the tape recorder. The clipping was of Noah, in firefighting gear, hanging by one arm from a collapsed fire escape, in his other hand he clutched a woman as smoke and flames billowed from an apartment window. The tip of a ladder was visible at the bottom of the frame. Noah remembered the incident and the shoulder and back pain that still remained.

"That woman, Noah, is my mother, she's alive today because of you."

The interrogator paused and locked eyes with Noah.

"It's a small world, isn't it?"

"You must be Deacon, Deacon Mobley, you came to see me in the hospital after the fire, you said you were going into the Army if I recall, man, you've had a growth spurt."

"My mother would never forgive me if anything bad ever happened to you on my account, and I have never, and never will, lie to my mother, by omission or otherwise."

"Yeah, it's a small world, but what now?"

"There are some people waiting outside for you Noah, they'll explain where you're going next."

The interrogator shook Noah's hand and opened the interview room door to let the Marine guard in. The guard unlocked Noah's handcuffs and his leg shackles and led him to an exit door where Mary Regis O'Malley and her brothers stood, a black SUV with tinted windows behind them.

"Well, look at this, three shanty Irish booze hounds sent to greet me."

Mary Regis hugged Noah, she hugged his bony frame with all her might and pushed her lips into the hollow of his face.

She stepped back, the sun shining on the wash of freckles about her nose and cheeks, her light brown hair swung in the wind. Tears ran from the corners of both eyes.

"Guess we'll need to fatten ye up – ye skinny fook."

THE ORACLE OF THE GAGRAS

THE GEORGIAN REGION OF THE RUSSIAN EMPIRE
AT THE MOUTH OF THE VERYOVKINA CAVE
JUNE 30, 1908

Ivan Aranofsky was exhausted from the climb, though not a steep one, it had proved long and arduous. Now, at over fifty years of age, he was feeling the effects of persistent arthritis. His joints ached and his mood darkened with every step. As a fact finder for the Royal Court, Ivan had been assigned to investigate the reports of prophesies fed to the people of the Caucusus through the mouth of an eight year old boy, the son of a shepherd.

Ivan felt it odd that religion can so many times be polluted by mysticism. Those professing to speak in tongues and to heal by faith have harmed so many, but yet we still wish to believe, we still wish to become part of a miracle.

Joining Professor Aranofsky on this expedition were members of the Royal Council of Sciences, representatives from the Orthodox Church of Russia, a conclave of Imams, and a group of Rabbis. Their presence requested by the boy, now known as the Oracle of the Gagras. In the Caucusus, there was a mix of religions and ethnicities, and for the most part, they existed without grievance. Maybe, thought Ivan, at some equilibrium of logic, they accepted that their individual beliefs and customs all flowed from the same fountainhead.

The party came to a halt before the mouth of a cave. After the tents were pitched and fires were ready to be built in anticipation of night, the boy, the Oracle, walked from the cave, accompanied by his parents and the village priest. He walked slowly to a crudely fashioned throne and seated himself. The priest motioned for all those in attendance to be silent, and to seat themselves on the ground, as near to the boy as possible. The boy's parents followed suit.

The boy closed his eyes and remained silent, waiting for the last mumble of those in attendance to cease. The priest lit torches on either side of the throne and then kneeled in front of the young prophet.

Ivan was curious as to what he would experience next. Would the young seer channel the dead, would he warn of an apocalypse, would he claim to be a Messiah, or would he simply make predictions so far into the future that he could not be held accountable for them in the present. And the motive for this charade could only be the benefits his family and the village priest would enjoy from this evening's farce. Gifts, respect, a new found sense of stature in the peasant community – a painfully simple motive Ivan could not ignore. As a man of science, he would view what unfolded through a prism of healthy skepticism.

The boy's eyes were closed, yet they twitched rapid fire as he grasped the arms of the throne. A light fog began to settle in as nighttime was imminent, creating a disturbing torch-lit diorama on the mountain side. A grey haze began to exit the cave. Ivan thought at first it was smoke, but there was no odor, just the haze which surrounded the throne and the boy with only his head and shoulders now visible.

And then the boy spoke. It was a booming voice, a voice to be respected, a voice that could not be ignored. It was as inspiring as it was frightening.

"In the past I have warned you of earthquakes and flooding, how to combat disease and aggression, what crops to plant and when to reap them, but tonight I will not speak to any of that, tonight I must inform you that I will speak to you no more, for after tonight, I must rest."

Ivan thought this an odd pronouncement. He hushed the rest of his contingent who were audibly puzzled as well.

163

The boy waited until his audience fell silent once again.

"I am not your God, I am not a god or a prophet, I am the sum total of you, your fears and aspirations, your courage, your successes and failures, your past, present, and future. Tell your men of faith and science that you are all connected and there is no insignificance in anything you do. The smallest of raindrops, the smallest of tears, the joy laughter brings, and the sadness when death beckons, you are all connected through the insignificant, you are all one. Centuries ago, after a great flood, a boat came to rest here, drawn to this point by the human spirit. To this day, I am the repository for that spirit, I am the collective consciousness of humanity, but after tonight I must rest. After I leave and before the sun rises you will witness something never witnessed before, a blue sun will appear above you in the evening sky, and it will progress thousands of miles away from here, in a matter of seconds, to the mouth of the Tunguska River, and the horizon will then appear as a new dawn. Let this become the dawn of a new mankind, a mankind that need not look to the skies for answers, but only into themselves, for it is there that all answers reside, and let it be known that the human spirit, the collectiveness that dwells in each and every one of you, has averted a planet killing disaster through benevolence and altruism."

The haze receded back into the mouth of the cave, the boy opened his eyes, his parents and the priest rose and stood alongside the makeshift throne. The entourage before them remained seated, confused, and silent.

And then the sound of thunder, the sky illuminated by a bright blue orb, a downdraft blew out the torches on either side of the throne, those who tried to stand were forced to the ground by a gale force wind. Then another sound, akin to the reverberation generated by cannon fire, and then the trembling of the earth underneath them. The entrance to the cave collapsed, covered in rubble. And off to the distance, what appeared to be the rising of a sun, as another sun began to set in the opposite direction.

Ivan struggled to his aching knees. This could not be, he thought, this simply cannot be. His suspicions peaked – had they been drugged by the water supplied to them, was the grey haze some form of hallucinogen, was an explosive triggered in the cave – this must be some elaborate magic trick or mass hysteria. He would need to take the boy with him, he would be the weakest link in this chain of deceit and trickery. He would pry the answers from the boy by any means necessary.

After a sleepless night of speculation on the mountain side, Ivan was eager to speak to the boy and his parents. They had slipped away down the mountain by torch light during the confusion, but Ivan was confident they had returned to the village below to destroy any evidence of their deception. The rest of the spectators were mixed in their reaction to the events of the evening before. Those of faith were convinced they had witnessed a miracle, those of science hypothesized they had witnessed a meteor enter the atmosphere, but how the boy knew it would happen was a mystery, a mystery they would solve through investigation and empirical evidence.

Early the following morning, Ivan visited the boy and his parents at their home. Ivan was accompanied by two Cossack guards, detailed to him from the Tsar's security force. Ivan was surprised to discover that the boy was apparently deaf. He had been since birth.

Pavel, the boy, communicated with his parents through a simple form of sign language. Although frustrated by this revelation, it would not deter Ivan's investigation or quell his cynicism. Ivan convinced the family, and later the priest, to travel with him back to St.Petersburg as it was their duty to do so, hinting that retribution would be swift if they chose not to.

The Tsarina would want to question them personally. Her keen interest in this case had driven Ivan to this primitive hut, it had driven him to cajole and threaten this family, the poorest of the poor, all to appease a monarch who was detached from her kingdom by arrogance and superstition.

First, a barrage of tests to determine if the boy actually was a mute, or if his parents had developed a form of ventriloquism which allowed them to speak through him. It all proved fruitless. The boy was questioned and pressured daily to reveal his secrets, but he remembered nothing of his encounters on the mountain or his prophesies. His parents were convinced their son was blessed by innocence and profound faith. They were simple people now caught up in a world they didn't understand.

After a year in St. Petersburg, the boy and his parents were allowed to return home. Advisors to the Tsar had cautioned that the oligarchs were growing weary of the Tsarina's obsession with what they perceived to be occult matters. No miracles had been performed, and no predictions had been made. The boy and his parents died a year later when a typhoid epidemic spread through their village unchecked. The priest remained in St. Petersburg, under the auspices of the Orthodox Church. Ivan thought it best to separate the foursome. Court advisors wanted no more tales of miracles or divine intervention, there was enough tension in the Empire without promises from duplicitous wise men and prophets.

It would be more than a decade before an expedition could be mounted to explore the event at Tunguska due to political upheaval and famine. In the short term, some of the native Ekeni were brought to St. Petersburg to tell their eyewitness accounts of the explosion and the aftermath before the Council of Sciences. Ivan thought it curious that these eyewitnesses all testified that herds of animals, and even birds, migrated away from the Tunguska region in the weeks before the explosion, this done in juxtaposition to their normal habits. The Ekeni interpreted this as an omen and scattered as well. The area was heavily forested and sparsely populated, perhaps no better place on earth to encounter such an explosion with such little loss of life.

Ivan Aranofsky was exiled to a Siberian prison camp after the Bolsheviks seized power, ironically, the closest he would ever come to Tunguska. He was an old man, crippled by arthritis and the ruminations of his experience in the Gagra Mountains. How can this be, he thought, how can such cruelty exist in the face of what the Oracle had told him. He would die of starvation within a few weeks of his imprisonment. Other prisoners would tear his clothes from his lifeless corpse, hoping to shield themselves from the cold before their own deaths would arrive.

It was nearly seventy years before the Veryovkina Cave was unearthed, explored, and mapped. Tales of the Gagras Oracle had been erased from recent memory and confined to folklore and the visions of future prophets. Tales of hope and peace that once ran rampant through the Caucusus were replaced by the specter of authoritarianism and blind obedience.

The first excavation at the cave revealed the bones of a child, seated in the rotting remains of a would-be throne. The miners from Ukraine and Poland who had been ordered to assist with the excavations stood in awe of this unearthed skeleton. They would return home with an infection of the mind and soul, they would display symptoms of hope and benevolence for the rest of their unusually long lives. This disease would spread quickly through family and countrymen, linking them together in the collective consciousness of humanity.

TIME, DISTANCE, AND SHIELDING

ST. ANTHONY'S ACADEMY
DEMOLITION SITE
1987

Noah Gregory followed the engine out of Station #3 after hearing the address announced over the intercom. As a Fire Marshal, it was always an option for him to respond on calls out of suspicion or curiosity. Most often, he became useful due to short staffing. Stretching a hoseline or throwing a ladder with the assistance of an extra set of hands was always appreciated on the fireground. Firefighters took pride in compensating for their shortcomings, sometimes to their own detriment. They would not accept failure, even though it reinforced the status-quo attitude of those controlling the purse strings.

Arson fires had become frequent in recent years. Vacant buildings, and sometimes a whole block or two of them, burned to the ground. Most of these fires were attributed to squatters, gangs, and drug dealers seeking revenge. The owners of these properties were most often real estate development companies, located out of state, and sometimes out of the country. Interestingly enough, these companies were difficult to communicate with, but they were meticulous with keeping their derelict properties insured. Someone was making money on the fires, and no doubt, on the re-sale of the properties, now cleared and ready for construction.

City Hall didn't want to hear any suspicions directed at potential developers. Times were tough, jobs were few, and fortunately, there hadn't been any deaths associated with these conflagrations. Noah had marked numerous buildings for master stream operations only. Rank and file firefighters were always too aggressive when the flames were roaring, it made no difference if the buildings were occupied or not. The standing orders for events at these buildings were to create collapse zones, and implement defensive operations, no offensive tactics requiring entry into the buildings were to be allowed.

But today was different. The call information shouldn't have been a cause for suspicion or curiosity, or defensive operations. There was a smoldering pile of debris at the site of a school demolition, a school Noah attended and sometimes loved and sometimes hated. A nuisance call most often handled by one man and a fire extinguisher.

On this morning, Noah needed a diversion, a trip down memory lane before he went off duty. Off duty is often attributed to relaxation and leisure, but today that definition would be a misnomer, for he knew the next two days would be filled with fear and worry. The next 48 hours could be debilitating when you're craving a drink, and the news today would surely require more than one drink. It was going to take a river of booze to quell the anxiety ramping up within him now.

Prostate cancer, most likely terminal, and the only treatments available have a very low rate of improving quality of life, let alone saving a life. The doctor had his suspicions after he looked at the CAT scan and MRI. A biopsy was the only way to be certain. The doctor didn't pull any punches. Noah appreciated that form of communication – prepare for the worst, hope for the best.

"The only treatment available may be castration and hormone therapy, and that's not a cure, the hormone therapy can be awfully tough, let's just keep our fingers crossed until we get the biopsy results. It'll be a day or two, but I'll get right back to you."

Noah tried to distance himself from that visit, but this morning's phone call brought that memory rocketing through his brain once again. Hormone therapy is tough, huh, he thought, how about having your balls cut off before you reach the age of forty, tell me that's not for the faint of heart.

And then the phone call received on the Fire Marshal's office line. A phone call juxtaposed between eagerness and apprehension. Noah's heart crept into his throat.

"It's what we feared Noah, come in tomorrow and we'll discuss treatment options, I'm sorry."

"Not as sorry as I am Doc." Noah slammed the receiver down as the announcement for the fire at the demolition site was broadcast over the intercom.

Noah sat parked in the Marshal's wagon. The crew of Engine #3 was spreading out a pile of debris and wetting it down. Noah could smell the rancid odor of smoke, the type of smoke generated by plastics and synthetic materials. Everything was left in the building, none of it to be salvaged due to the EPA order, all of it to be removed to an EPA waste site for disposal. It could be anything burning, and none of it healthy for the human blood stream or lungs.

When Noah first hired on and his obsessive compulsive order would mount, he would often repeat a phrase his Battalion Chief told him during basic training.

"Time, distance, and shielding, that's the gospel for radiation, but we can apply that to anything hazardous – chemicals, diseases, and even smoke, we didn't give you thousands of dollars of equipment not to wear. So, gentlemen, repeat after me, limit time in hazardous atmospheres, maintain a safe distance from anything hazardous, and wear your turn out gear and air-pack in those atmospheres – the age of the smoke eater is dead for good reason."

Time, distance, and shielding, no better advice to someone afflicted with OCD. Time, distance, and shielding, thought Noah, music to my ears. And when Noah applied that advice to other facets of his life during times of strife and anxiety, his OCD became just a bit more tolerable, it was all more tolerable when he retreated into that bubble. Time, distance, and shielding – it became his mantra. He repeated it constantly, much like a prayer or a command. But, could he use it this time to build a force field to protect himself from the ravages of this disease sent to consume him. It was doubtful. He had used it for years to dodge the imaginary, reality was harsh, it was a stiff punch to the face.

In an act of defiance aimed at his own psyche, Noah rolled the window down on the Marshal's wagon to get a taste of the burning material. This done in direct opposition to his mantra. What does it matter now, he thought, what does it matter. Fuck the force field, nothing is going to kill me before the cancer, so what does it matter. No amount of repetition or a coping ritual is going to save me from it, so what the fuck does anything matter now.

"If you can see it, taste it, or smell it, fill out an exposure report."

More sage advice to Noah from the Battalion Chief during training, but there would be no exposure reports filed today. What does it matter now, he thought. The engine crew didn't even bother to don air-packs or protective gear, so more power to them. They'll take a bath in that shit and probably be no worse for wear while I'll be six feet under. Good for them.

The school and the nearby convent were found to be sitting on an old chemical dump, with unacceptable mercury and benzene levels. The EPA discovered a cluster of cancer cases related to students and citizens in the immediate neighborhood a few years prior to the order to raze the building and neighboring homes. The next steps would be excavation and encasement. Those suffering the effects of the hazards were warned it might take years and a few class action suits before they saw a dime of compensation. Great, thought Noah, I'll be dead long before then, along with everyone else who absorbed the carcinogens, what an epitaph for a Catholic school founded on hope and faith.

And when that last shovel full of dirt fills my grave, a lawyer will rush to my graveside with evidence that it was the chemicals that did me in, but my mother and daughter will be ineligible for any compensation because I'm already gone. That's the way it goes, he thought, that's the way it goes.

"The simplest solution is the correct one."

Noah's childhood friend would often repeat that when something became glaringly apparent. For some reason, Noah often dreamt of that friend, Alvin Bean, who was as crazy as he was funny, and never at a loss for a theory or a flat out lie. What the hell Alvin, what if there are no solutions?

And the dreams about Alvin made no sense, most of them were disconcerting, and when he wanted to stop dreaming, he just kicked his alcohol abuse into high gear, and when it was in high gear, it was not an enjoyable environment for his wife, now his ex, or his daughter. But the dreams about Alvin Bean had become psychologically draining, realistic and haunting. Alvin wanted something from Noah in those dreams, and he wasn't going to stop until he got it.

Noah was about to return to the station when he felt a hand on his arm through the driver's side window.

"Hey, Mr. DiFabio, how are you?"

Tony DiFabio had been the head of maintenance at St. Anthony's all through Noah's attendance. A genuine nice guy who the students loved and respected, although the missing fingers on his right hand were impossible to ignore, even now.

"Brings back memories Noah, don't you think."

"Sure does, but some of them aren't so nice."

Noah looked down at Tony's maimed hand, now on his arm. It felt red hot, the heat ran like an electrical current through Noah's biceps and shoulders, down through his abdomen, through his legs and into his feet.

"Sorry Noah, I forgot you don't like to be touched."

Tony drew his hand away and leaned down to be face to face with Noah.

"It's not that Mr. D, your hand feels like you're burning up, do you feel alright, you need a lift to Urgent Care?"

"Nah, I'm okay, I just run hot, that's what the doctors say, but I saw you sitting here, and you kinda' looked out of sorts, like you used to when you first came to St. Anthony's, so I thought I'd give you a cheer up like the old days."

Noah smiled, Mr. D always had an array of corny jokes and a pocketful of hard candies to dole out to those feeling "out of sorts," but a joke or a butterscotch candy wouldn't help today, but the memory did, and Noah appreciated that.

"Look at you, the man with two first names is a fire department Captain, and not just any Captain, you carry a weapon to keep the city safe, I bet your mom is proud."

"Well the baseball thing didn't work out as you probably know."

"There are no guarantees Noah, but everything happens for a reason. You got to the minor leagues, but look at you now, you're what every young boy wants to be, and what every old man wishes he could have been, don't be so hard on yourself."

Yeah, thought Noah, but no boy or old man would want his balls chopped off, but he shook his head and smiled back at Tony DiFabio.

"I like being a firefighter as much as playing ball, and it does pay a hell of a lot more than the minor leagues did."

"But ballplayers don't save lives, you guys make a difference, don't forget that."

"Hey, Mr. D, this isn't the healthiest place to be you know, lots of bad stuff in the ground here."

"I spent 35 years here Noah, what's going to get me now?"

"You've got a point, did you finally retire?"

"Nah, I'd be bored silly, took a job at the nursing facility on Mohawk Avenue, nice place, no pressure, couldn't believe what the pay was. I'm on my way there now, thought it would be a nice day for a walk."

"Good for you Mr. D, take it while you can, but you're welcome to a ride if you'd like."

"Thanks Noah, but I think I'll spend a few minutes here watching the tear down before I meander into work."

Noah put the station wagon in gear. The firefighters were packing the hose back onto the truck, so he couldn't justify hanging out at the demolition site any longer, but then again he thought, what would it matter.

"Watch yourself Mr. D, I've got to get back to the station."

Tony DiFabio took a step back and turned towards the remains of St. Anthony's Academy. He situated his hands on his hips and sighed.

As Noah stopped his vehicle before turning onto the street, a figure approached him through the gate of the chain link fence which surrounded the demolition site. A man in coveralls and wearing a welder's visor. Probably the guy who set the pile on fire while cutting metal, probably wants to know if he's going to get ticketed thought Noah.

Noah put the station wagon in park and rolled the driver's side window down all the way. No harm, no foul, he thought, that's what I'll tell this guy, no harm, no foul, just be more careful next time. The man approached, his visor still down, and handed Noah a small metal box before turning away. Noah examined the box, a pencil box, he remembered those from elementary classes. On the box, a replica of Carl Yaztremski's rookie card that looked peculiarly familiar to Noah. He shook the box, something inside made the sound of metal on metal. He opened the box to discover the only content was one large framing nail.

Then, the ugly memory of his biological father driving an identical nail through a leather belt and then into the casing above a doorway, and then the memory of his father swinging by the neck from that belt. It had been years since Noah relived that memory, how did that son-of-a-bitch know.

Noah slammed the vehicle into park and hurried through the gate and into the restricted area to find the welder, but he wasn't to be seen.

"Where'd that guy go wearing the welder's helmet," Noah stopped the first worker he approached.

"Took off on a bicycle, was in here milling about when the foreman told him to beat it."

Noah looked up and down the street, but no bicycles were in sight. A practical joke from the engine company maybe, there's a chance they knew about Noah's beginnings, after all he was adopted by a firefighter after the incident, but then again no, they'd never do anything to sully the image of that man, he was referred to with the reverence due a Saint.

"Well, fuck it," he murmured to himself, "what does it matter now, what does it matter now."

The station wagon crawled down Madison Avenue on course for the station. Tony DiFabio waved to Noah as he drove by, but Noah didn't notice, he was caught between fear and bewilderment, and only alcohol could fix what he was experiencing.

"Time, distance, and shielding," he whispered, "put up that force field and never let it down."

FAKE JESUS

THE BAR & GRILL
HALLOWEEN
1981

Noah Gregory was in the midst of being persuaded by the firefighters on his shift to attend the Halloween party at Charlie Cossack's Bar & Grill. Noah sat on the bumper of the engine. The overhead door was open, letting in the cool autumn air after a day of sunshine and moderate temperatures. Leonard was anxious to get to the party. He paced back and forth, hoping the relief crew would arrive before another alarm came in. It had been a busy tour of duty.

Since Noah's wife had abandoned him and their infant daughter a year ago, there had been no time for entertainment or relaxation. His focus had been directed upon his daughter and widowed mother to the point of obsession. Obsession to the point of compulsion, the anomalous demons he had been battling to a standstill for most of his life. The demons which still roamed the darkest hallways of his mind, always just one thought away.

His shift mates tried to cajole him into the outing with promises of scantily clad women and cheap drinks. But there was a danger in tonight's outing, his drinking had been under control for the better part of three years, he had mastered moderation, it would be foolish to blow all of that now.

"Come on Noah, what the hell, it'll be a good time," Leonard urged, "after this tour of duty we all need some R and R."

"Do we need costumes – I'm not dressing up."

"We'll just wear our uniforms, might get us a free drink or two."

Leonard persisted, he was sure Noah could be convinced to join them.

"Listen, I promise we'll get out of there early, but you're gonna' love it, I went last year and the bartenders were the chicks from the strip club down the street and they were all in bikinis, and there was a wet t-shirt contest at the end of the night, it was nuts."

That sealed the deal. Noah called his mother to tell her he would be late and to plan on keeping Marta, his daughter, for another night.

So, five firefighters from Station 3 walked the four city blocks to the Bar & Grill, hell bent on a night of some much needed boozing and depravity.

"This better be worth it Leonard, this place doesn't look so great from the outside."

Noah eyed the front façade of the building as the rest of his crew made their way to the door.

There was a bouncer at the door checking IDs and taking the cover charge. He was a large man and dressed in what appeared to be a bear suit. There were stains down the front of it and the zipper was pulled apart from the neck to the bouncer's abdomen. He eyed the firefighters from head to toe.

"You guys real firemen?"

"Sure are," Leonard answered, a smile stretched across his slender face.

"No charge, you guys good."

"What did I tell you Noah, we're golden here."

Leonard squeezed his way to the bar through the blue pall of cigarette smoke and costumed attendees.

"I'll order us some beers."

Noah took a look around. Leonard was right, the bar was packed, and many of the attendees were young women, many of them dressed suggestively as street walkers or movie stars. There was something about Halloween that brought that out in women. An excuse to be the opposite of what they had to portray in everyday life. And, as promised, the bartenders were in bikinis, and they were loud and at any given moment they sprayed customers with seltzer bottles and challenged them to do shots with them. A sign behind the bar offered free drinks to any woman daring to dance on the bar, and if she were to throw her bra into the crowd, her entire party could drink for free. One drunken young woman fell as she tried to stand on the bar, her bra in hand, the crowd shielded her fall and gave her a rousing ovation.

Leonard passed beers from the bar to where his shift mates stood.

"They're on the house Noah, what'd I tell you, this is great, huh?"

Noah didn't reply, he spotted Charlie Cossack at the end of the bar, dressed in a tuxedo. Next to him stood another man, every bit as large as the bouncer, dressed as a referee, a whistle hung from a lanyard around his neck.

"Where you headed Noah?"

Noah didn't answer, he squeezed through the crowd, towards the end of the bar, beer in hand.

"Well, if it's not the man with two first names, how the hell have you been?"

Charlie Cossack reacted to the firefighter who stood before him and shook his hand.

"Not too bad, haven't seen you since high school, who are you supposed to be?"

"Bond, James Bond."

Charlie tried his best for a British accent.

"Heard you bought this place, sort of like your own den of

inequity, huh?"

Charlie smiled at that remark and finished what was in the shot glass he held.

"Once a year we cut loose, otherwise the place is usually dead except for a few regulars," Charlie glanced over Noah's shoulder and towards the door before he continued, "working for a company out of Toronto, we do entertainment, and real estate, with a market to small and medium size cities, might dip our toes into the insurance business soon."

"How'd you wind up in Toronto?"

"Some of my family up there got hold of me after my dad was killed in the rail yards, an uncle, more like a great uncle, how about you, last I knew you were playing in the minors."

"Yeah, that didn't work out so well, but this firefighter job is a good gig, came here with a few buddies on my shift."

"Good, glad to hear it, didn't you marry Gretchen Moss, thought I saw in the paper you two got married at home plate in Elmira."

"Not anymore, she left me for Larry Flowers."

"Fat Larry – never could stand that son-of-a-bitch, you should've taken the money we offered you to throw her off a bridge, no offense, but I couldn't stand her either."

The baseball team at St. Anthony's Academy did jokingly offer Noah a coffee can full of money if he would do something ugly to Gretchen. He laughed it off at the time, but they saw what he didn't. He was blinded by the booze, the pot, and the teenage sex she offered. The ultimate masquerade perpetrated by a narcissist. His teammates saw her for what she was, a manipulative, mean spirited woman, with a personality disorder which would only ferment with age.

"No offense taken, but you can't hurt a girl, right Charlie?"

"Yeah, you're right on that, once they start with the tears they own you."

"Whatever happened to Dagger Lorow," Noah took a sip of his beer, it tasted too good, this could be a long night.

"He's a prison guard in California."

"A prison guard – must be they don't check for criminal records out there."

Charlie nodded his head in agreement and laughed.

"Must be."

Charlie looked over Noah's shoulder again and then motioned for the bartender to cut off the juke box.

"I've got to handle something Noah, you and your guys drink for free tonight, we'll catch up later."

Charlie maneuvered his way to the door where a man dressed as Jesus stood. He was accompanied by two women dressed as Playboy Bunnies. The referee followed Charlie.

The bar grew silent, all eyes were on Charlie and the robed man who stood with a cardboard cross behind him. It was attached to his waist by a cord, he held onto the cross handles with outstretched arms. The bunnies giggled as Charlie approached.

"You think you're fucking funny?"

Charlie was livid, the bouncer and the referee stood on either side of him.

The fake Jesus didn't respond.

"I asked you a fucking question – do you think you're funny asshole?"

"Listen, it's just a joke."

The string holding the beard to fake Jesus' face was apparent as he spoke.

"Well here's another joke motherfucker."

Charlie delivered a swift, crisp, punch to his adversary's nose. Fake Jesus reeled backwards and one knee buckled from the blow. He cupped the blood flowing from his nostrils with both hands.

Charlie nodded to the giants on either side of him. They ripped the cardboard cross from the back of the fake Jesus and took hold of him by the arms and legs. They opened the doors with his head, as if he was a battering ram, and threw him from the sidewalk into the road. The Playboy Bunnies who accompanied him rushed to his side and started to drag him from the roadway and back onto the sidewalk.

Inside, Charlie motioned to the bartender and the music was back on, blaring once again, as Charlie tossed the cardboard cross out the door. The giants re-entered, the one in the bear suit closed the door behind him and resumed his duties checking IDs and taking admission fees.

"What the hell was that all about?"

Leonard stood elbow to elbow with Noah.

"I guess you can take the boy out of St. Anthony's, but you can't take the St. Anthony's out of the boy."

Noah didn't expect anything less from Charlie. Tonight was shaping up to be exactly how Leonard had predicted.

BACKGROUND MUSIC

TWO MONTHS AFTER THE DEATH OF TONY DIFABIO
UTICA, NY

Hannigan Butler awoke to the glare of sunshine tearing through the bed sheet nailed across the bedroom window. His head pounded from the night before. Nausea coursed through his chest as he positioned himself in a seated position on the edge of the bed. His girlfriend Wendy laid face down, a sheet partly draped over her naked ass, stopping just short of her greasy blonde hair.

Hannigan stumbled into the bathroom clad in black dress socks, nothing else. He knelt and clung to the toilet. He needed to vomit, which he did, over and over until the dry heaves took hold. After a few minutes he was able to stand and lean against the bathroom sink and stare into the mirror above it.

The whites of his eyes were crimson from the blood vessels ruptured during his morning ritual of vomiting and fainting, vomiting and fainting. Most often he would crawl back into bed, a wastebasket placed alongside the bed for assurances sake. He always checked the remains of his fountain of bile for blood, a sure sign of esophageal ruptures, which would be the harbinger of death. The jaundice was starting to return. Unnoticeable to most, but he could see the initial tell tale signs in his eyes, when not blood-shot from the dry heaves, and his nail beds. It had always dissipated with a few weeks of sobriety, fluids, and healthy meals, but Hannigan was unsure if he had a few weeks left, let alone a few weeks to spare.

Sobriety was always on the to-do list, maybe a stay at a rehab center, maybe just rock hard determination and unflappable will, and ironically, maybe a miracle. He had been investigating and debunking miracles for the past five years, but now it seemed a miracle would be the only thing to save his life from the endless cycle of addictions and the miseries they ushered forth. He never met a drug or an alcohol he didn't fall in love with along with the nearest enabler who now slept beside him.

Today was different. In order to be paid for his latest investigation into what many believed was a case of spontaneous human combustion, Hannigan would need to visit Sister Jude at the St. Vincent Hospice Center. And in order to do so, he would need to display a demeanor of self confidence, and the appearance of competence. A tall order for the wretch he had become.

He was in desperate need of money. Since Wendy had been fired from the bar, he could no longer drink for free thanks to her bartending and careful work at the cash register. She was a master at short changing drunks and selling them unfulfilled promises of sexual gratification. She was a charlatan, a grifter, and a talented thief and pick-pocket. But that all ended when her boss, Charlie Cossack, announced her employment was over, and she was forbidden to ever darken the doorway of the Bar & Grill again.

Whenever high or drunk, or both, Hannigan felt invincible. When he sobered up after a binge, the insecurities arrived along with a peculiar paranoia. Hannigan was convinced others could sense his fear and confusion, they could sense them by taste or smell, he was sure he carried that aroma. It was the only explanation for complete strangers to confront him with their accusations, their confessions, their observations about him.

Two days prior, Hannigan had phoned the Bishop's office about payment for his investigation into the fire at the skilled nursing facility. If he wanted his money, he was informed he would need to pick it up in person. Many in the community had attributed the fire to a miracle, the arrival of the Holy Spirit, triggered by a white cardinal that had been making appearances at the windowsill of the victim. The locals wanted to believe the fire was divine, the bird's arrival and its persistence in visiting the comatose patient's room was a prophecy.

Although a rarity, the appearance of an albino bird, or any other creature lacking skin pigmentation, was not unique in Hannigan's mind. As often was the case, the locals created their own lore about the fire and the bird. A prayer group would meet in the courtyard of the facility to offer prayers for their sick and loved ones. And any events that followed were attributed to miracles generated by a comatose man named Alvin Bean. They truly believed the bird to be a sign of hope and charity, delivered to them by the shell of a poor human being, bed-ridden and unconscious for months after being struck by a vehicle while riding his bicycle.

The Fire Marshal's Office had ruled the cause of the fire as undetermined after the State Police Lab could not definitely state that the damage to the motor powering the victim's bed was from an external or internal source. Hannigan's own investigation stated that although the cause could not be proven to a scientific certainty, it was inconceivable that the victim had spontaneously ignited, and therefore, the motor was the cause. In reality, Hannigan was hoping he could be paid as an expert witness if subrogation arose between the bed manufacturer and the nursing facility. It could be a great payday. A great payday if he was alive to enjoy it.

But then the wrench thrown into the gears. Tony DiFabio, a maintenance man at the nursing facility, and the last person to have seen the victim alive, died under mysterious circumstances as well. When Hannigan arrived at Mr. DiFabio's apartment to interview him, he found the apartment door slightly ajar. He peeked in and saw Mr. DiFabio standing and staring out the window adjacent to the efficiency kitchen. He was dressed in boxer shorts and a t-shirt, his complexion an eerie blue, but his eyes were wide open and covered in a milky glaze. He didn't respond to Hannigan's knocks at the door or his voice, so Hannigan stepped in, hoping not to frighten Tony, who might be hard of hearing. When Hannigan tapped him on the shoulder, he didn't move. He was lifeless, but it appeared he had died standing up, with wooden Rosary Beads wrapped around his disfigured right hand.

Hannigan dialed 911 from the wall phone adjacent to the kitchen.

"I don't know if this guy is alive or dead, but someone needs to check this out."

When the ambulance crew arrived, they stood in awe before arguing about how to remove Mr. DiFabio from the apartment and down the long, narrow stairwell.

"We're gonna snap this guy in half, and after all this might be a crime scene, not an unattended death."

"We shouldn't be moving dead people anyway," the other medic chimed in.

The crew leader decided upon caution, but allowed Hannigan to remain on the scene while they reached out to the coroner's office.

Noah Gregory, a Fire Marshal, responded to the scene in the minutes before the coroner arrived. Hannigan had spoken to Captain Gregory about interviewing Mr. DiFabio a few days prior to today's event.

"Captain, we're waiting for the coroner, this is just too plain weird for us to move this guy."

A medic acknowledged the Captain's arrival.

"Yeah, I heard it come over the radio, thought I'd check it out – you just can't make this shit up, can you?"

Noah and Hannigan made eye contact. The corpse remained standing as the medics argued about their next course of action.

The coroner arrived and asked the medics to transport the deceased to the hospital morgue for an autopsy to determine the cause of death. There were no apparent signs of foul play or suicide. It was an ugly and clumsy scene as the medics decided to carry Mr. DiFabio down the stairs, a stretcher or a back board wouldn't fit in the stairwell, and sitting this mannequin of a corpse in a chair for removal was beyond acceptable.

Hannigan and Noah turned their heads, unable to watch this chaos cloaked in comedy. It's a human defense to find humor in grotesque tragedy, a defense mechanism familiar to both Noah and Hannigan.

In the weeks that followed, the spiral of addiction did its best to consume Hannigan. When the alcohol wasn't enough he snorted enough cocaine to down a grizzly bear. And in the process, a gusher of a nose bleed soiled his only clean dress shirt.

He'd need to buy another before meeting Sister Jude to pick up his check. He crawled out of bed again and donned pants and shoes along with a nylon wind breaker. His vehicle had stopped running a day ago, a dead battery which he could not afford, so it would be a long walk to J.C. Penney's and then to the hospice center. He rifled through Wendy's purse and found a couple five dollar bills. She'd been holding out again as usual. He donned his sunglasses from the shelving next to the door and decided it would be a good idea to eat before starting his journey, the pizza joint across the street would have to do.

He ordered a slice of cheese pizza and grabbed a bottle of soda from the cooler and then seated himself.

An employee approached him with his order. A young man with bushy red hair and bulging eyes. His baseball cap was ill fitting, and he appeared angry.

"Here's your pizza mister, but you should've ordered the breakfast pizza, that was my invention."

"Really, that's served all over town, so I'm not so sure you invented it."

"Oh yeah, I invented the pineapple pizza too, and someone stole that idea too."

"You know what kid, why don't you just leave me alone, I'm feeling a little under the weather."

"That's the problem with people, they don't want to hear the truth, and I'll tell you something else, that son-of-a-bitch Charlie Cossack stole the spaghetti sandwich idea from me too."

That name again, it was central to every strange thing Hannigan had encountered since arriving in Utica for the fire investigation.

"Hey Banjo Eyes, leave the customer alone and get your ass back in the kitchen," a voice boomed from behind the counter.

The employee retreated back towards the kitchen as Hannigan took a bite of the pizza. It wasn't going to work, he'd never get it down, let alone keep it down, but he'd take the soda with him and sip on it, maybe it would calm the nausea.

It was close to a half an hour walk to the nearest J.C. Penney store. It was humid and Hannigan perspired underneath the wind breaker he wore. He'd need to put the shirt on at the store once he bought it. A plain white shirt and a solid color tie would do. He still had a J.C. Penney card, all his others had been canceled due to non-payment. Then a cab ride to the hospice center, that would be the plan.

Hannigan sorted through the dress shirts, looking for his size, something plain, something cheap.

"Excuse me, try these on for me, will you, you're about my husband's size."

A middle aged woman wearing too much makeup stood next to Hannigan, a pile of shirts draped over her arm.

"I can tell you my size if that helps."

"Come on, try them on will you?"

"Listen lady, I'm not putting on a fashion show here, got it?"

"Well fuck you then."

The woman tossed the shirts onto a nearby table and walked towards the exit. It was happening again, no doubt, Hannigan was convinced she could smell the aroma of fear and confusion that enveloped him.

He purchased his items and asked the sales girl if he could change into them in the dressing room. She just shrugged and pointed to their direction.

Hannigan called a cab from the payphone in front of the store and seated himself on the bench next to it. A young woman seated herself next to Hannigan. Much too close to him. It felt awkward. She would at times take a small notebook from her purse and jot something down in it with a sharpened pencil. She was slim and dressed in business attire. She focused her gaze straight ahead with teary eyes. After writing in her notebook she would toss the pencil to the ground and pull out another from her purse, just as sharp as the previous one.

That pencil would make a formidable weapon. One quick swing and it could be in Hannigan's neck or eye. Hannigan was about to stand when the woman rose and walked away. She left behind a piece of paper with the word "MISANTHROPE" written upon it.

He had reached a new level of uneasiness. He hoped it was just a form of drug induced paranoia, the kind that would fade as the drug wore off. He tried to compose himself during the cab ride. But why this Sister Jude, and why at a hospice center?

The hospice center was a narrow, three story building with screened in porches on every level. It was originally built to house TB patients, the porches were for fresh air, a treatment for those suffering from the disease. It was painted a bright white which reflected the morning sunlight directly into Hannigan's face as he climbed the front concrete steps.

Hannigan was led to see Sister Jude by a nun wearing a medical smock. The answer as to why he was meeting her here soon became clear. She was a patient. She sat alone on the second story porch facing the street. Around her face and attached to her nose was nasal tubing supplying oxygen to her ravaged body. Next to her on a small table was an ashtray, cigarette butts spilled out from it. She was dressed in a dark blue bath robe, a habit covered her head. She held a pack of cigarettes in one hand and a lighter in the other.

The escort exited the porch leaving Sister Jude and Hannigan to talk. There were no introductions or pleasantries exchanged.

"It's lung cancer, but I still smoke because this form of lung cancer isn't caused by cigarettes, probably environmental, probably from the convent they're tearing down."

"I'm sorry to hear that Sister."

"Are you really? I think you just need money, just look at you, you couldn't even muster the energy to shave, and what are you hiding behind those sunglasses, and I can smell the booze on you even with this tubing in my nose."

"My appearance is beside the point, I completed the investigation and submitted a report as requested, Alvin Bean's death was caused by an overheated motor in his hospital bed, and the coroner's report attributed the death of Tony DiFabio to a lethal arrhythmia, severe arthritis and rigor mortis is what led to finding him standing up, there were no miracles, just two weird coincidences."

"You'll get your money Mr. Butler, but first I need to tell you how bad you are at simple math."

"What's math got to do with any of this?"

"You've ignored the common denominator here, the real miracle – Tony DiFabio may well be a Saint, that's what you've ignored, that's why you're here."

"I have no idea what you're talking about."

"Maybe you should have attended Tony's funeral, you could have met the Filipino priest who maintains that Tony healed his wounds by prayer alone after he was bayoneted, or the Japanese soldiers who dropped their weapons and helped Tony and the priest escape the Death March."

"That makes him a Saint, because he survived being a prisoner of war?"

"No, what makes him a Saint are the miracles I suspect him of here in Utica."

"Alvin Bean goes up in flames, how can a tragic event like that be considered a miracle?"

"I'm talking about three miracles I witnessed as a social worker at St. Miriam's Hospital when Tony would visit the hospital and say the Rosary for those receiving the Last Rites."

"I wasn't hired to investigate any of that, I had no need to look into that."

"But you should have, Tony was the background music, the soundtrack for the appearance of the white cardinal at the nursing facility, I'm certain of that."

"That bird again, what is it with you people, it's just an albino bird."

"I'm going to leave you with three names and some advice before I hand you the check today Mr. Butler."

Sister Rene paused to calm her breathing and ease the high pitched wheezing that was coming with her every word.

"I was a social worker at the hospital as I told you, and I

witnessed Tony DiFabio heal three children by prayer alone. Charlie Cossack, I'm sure you're familiar with that name, dying from an advanced case of Whooping Cough, Naomi Clearwater, who was in an iron lung from a severe case of Polio, and Lili-Che Faithful, thought to be brain dead after a car accident, and as far as I know, they are all alive and well today, although some would argue Charlie Cossack isn't so well, but miracles don't discriminate, they happen for a reason, and we should never question those reasons."

Sister Jude's breathing became rapid and labored.

"What about Alvin Bean, him catching on fire was beneficial for him?"

"Somehow it freed him from the prison of his own body, and in doing so in such a dramatic fashion, it set the stage for what will happen next, I'm sure of that."

"So, what's happening next?"

"I'm not sure Mr. Butler, but I do know miracles exist, Saints walk among us as well as those who have no souls, and you were drawn here for a reason, everything happens for a reason, and you need only listen to the background music to figure this all out, but you'll need to abandon cynicism and embrace faith in order to do so."

Sister Jude put her sleeve across her face and coughed. A deep, wet, raspy cough. The conversation had been robbing her of needed oxygen.

Hannigan crouched to receive the check Sister Jude pulled from the pocket of her bathrobe.

"Thank you Sister, I hope you feel better."

"That's not going to happen Mr. Butler, you know that, but I'm not afraid now that I've completed my piece of the puzzle."

Hannigan didn't unfold the check until he got a block away from the hospice center. It was a handsome amount. His next mission would be to find a nearby bank. His conversation with the nun had been strange, it filled him with a new sense of uncertainty which he couldn't blame on alcohol, drugs, or the pounding headache threatening to tear his skull to pieces. But a few drinks and a wallet full of cash would erase the uneasiness in short order, after all, a worthy investigator worships only at the altar of skepticism.

ASHES TO ASHES

THE NIGHT OF THE FIRE
UTICA, NY
1988

Naomi Clearwater stood outside and watched the flames pour from the broken showcase window. She had heard a rumble from the back of the bar before the fire tore through the rear office and kitchen. She sprayed the contents of a dry chemical extinguisher towards the direction of the flames to no avail. The four or five customers left at closing scattered into the safety of the street. One returned and carried her to safety. She fought her removal but was unsure why she had done so. Her objections were futile. The stranger who saved her was too strong and forceful. She looked for him in the street, but he was gone.

Something tore through her brain as she stood alongside the other bystanders being pushed back by the firefighters who were stretching hose lines into the front entry way. She gazed upon the door just to the left of the showcase windows. The door which led to the apartment she was staying in directly above the bar. All her belongings were there, she didn't have much, but they were all she had. It didn't appear that the fire had spread to the second floor, she might be able to make it and take what she needed. It was worth a try. It appeared the fire was darkening down. The firefighters were busy, they wouldn't notice if she scampered up the stairs. She just needed to punch in the numbers on the door lock and make a mad dash. She was sure she wouldn't be noticed.

The race was on. She was up the stairs in seconds, but the smoke was hot and dense. She got to her door, a flimsy hollow core door. Her keys were in her purse in the bar, so she gave the door a solid kick with the sole of her shoe and it swung open. The smoke was banking down towards the floor, her lungs were burning, but she needed to grab the backpack that hung from the coat rack mounted next to the door. She couldn't reason why that backpack seemed so important, she just needed to grab it. That backpack needed to be saved, she felt compelled to grab it and take it with her. Halfway down the stairs the hot, black smoke choked her into unconsciousness.

"You're a lucky woman Naomi."

She opened her eyes to see an ER physician standing over her.

To his side was Noah Gregory a city Fire Marshal who as of late had become one of her best customers at the bar.

Naomi's eyes were swollen from the heat and smoke and her face was covered by an oxygen mask.

"You risked it all to grab a backpack? You're just lucky a firefighter was detailed to search the second story or we would've been taking you to the morgue."

Captain Gregory moved closer, his tone was matter of fact, not an attempt at a lecture.

She pulled the oxygen mask to one side of her face to respond to the Captain.

"I'm not sure why I did it, the backpack doesn't even belong to me, it was there when I moved in."

She coughed and returned the mask to its proper position.

"You're not the only one, we've had people run back into burning buildings and come out with the TV Guide, not much sense to be made when you're in a panic."

A nurse entered and told Naomi she was going to draw blood to determine her carbon dioxide levels. It would be from an artery in her wrist and it would be painful.

"Listen," continued Noah, "when you're discharged, I'll need to talk to you about what happened, no hurry, when you feel up to it."

Naomi nodded and Noah turned to leave before facing her again.

"Any idea what was in the backpack?"

Naomi shook her head no.

Noah unzipped the backpack which was on a chair next to the stretcher.

"Just some composition notebooks, and thanks to you, they're in mint condition."

Noah zipped the backpack up and slung it over his shoulder.

"I'll give it to Charlie when I talk to him about all this."

Naomi nodded and then winced when the needle found the artery in her wrist.

She pulled the mask to one side once again.

"Tell Gennady I'm okay if you get a chance, he'll be worried."

Noah winked.

"Will do, get some rest."

Naomi found herself working at the bar after a chance encounter with Gennady some months earlier. He changed a tire for her on an isolated road in the heart of Pennsylvania and ended the good deed with an invitation for coffee.

She took him up on the offer and the relationship was kindled. Gennady thought it best not to mention where they had met to his employer Charlie Cossack. There had been an unsavory event that Naomi had been a party to that evening, and Charlie was better off not knowing who she was, or that she was there. Better to let sleeping dogs lie.

"You know I went to high school here for a short while when I was recovering from Polio, he might remember me, I remember him."

"If he remembers okay, just don't bring up the whole tire changing thing or that guy we dealt with."

Gennady's English was flawless, but it was punctuated by a thick eastern European accent which attracted Naomi to him in the first place.

Gennady, Bohdan, and Charlie were often absent from the bar, away on business as they would phrase it. The three of them planned to headquarter their business in Buffalo come the near future and Naomi was invited to join them if she so pleased, or she could remain in Utica and run the Bar & Grill.

In the meantime, she made the liquor and beer orders, kept the alley bird feeders full, and above all, made sure Charlie's inner and outer office doors remained locked. The day's receipts were always stuffed into a drop safe at the end of the night and she had the name of a cop to call if anyone got rowdy or she felt threatened. It didn't matter what time of day or for what, she was guaranteed he would come. She fell under Gennady's supervision, and he paid her twice what she should have been making. Once the tips were added in along with the use of the upstairs apartment for nothing, she had found a comfortable niche.

The relationship with Gennady grew, but he still insisted on keeping it quiet. She was unsure why because even a blind man could see the way he felt about her. But, she wasn't one to break her word and she valued his trust above all.

After getting chest x-rays, breathing treatments, and being pumped full of fluids in the ER, Naomi was moved to the ICU for observation. It was there that a doctor visited and gave her some unexpected news.

"Miss Clearwater, did you know you were pregnant?"

Naomi was stunned. Gennady had phoned the hospital a few hours prior to her receiving this news. She told him she was feeling fine, but now she had some life altering news to share with him.

He would be back in town in another day. Would he rejoice or would he be angry. In the months she had known him, he never appeared angry, but then again, when you're his size, people avoid making you angry at all costs.

As these thoughts tumbled through her mind, Captain Gregory paid another visit before her discharge.

"I've spoken to all the bystanders but one, the guy who pulled you out of the bar, any idea who he is, the other guys said they'd never seen him before."

"Me neither, big guy, black guy, quiet guy, but he looked like this boxer I've seen on TV if that helps."

Noah laughed.

"Saw some highlights of his fights one night in the bar, and he does a lot of ads now."

"I'll keep that in mind, need to make sure he had nothing to do with it, it was an arson job, somebody wrapped a small tank of propane with blasting caps and rolled it through the back door."

"They could have killed us."

So this is why Gennady wants to keep their relationship hush-hush, he doesn't want her to get hurt on his account.

"One more question Naomi, I remember you from St. Anthony's, you weren't there for very long, but you were in a wheelchair right, I've been trying to put it together where I've seen you before, but the wheelchair thing threw me."

"Yeah, they thought I had Polio, but when I recovered they said they weren't sure what the hell I had."

"You've never mentioned that."

"Gennady asked me not to."

"Don't worry, I won't bring it up either."

A nurse squeezed by Noah as he exited the room. She began disconnecting Naomi's IV lines.

"You're free to go Miss Clearwater, just follow up with your doctor next week, and Mr. Cossack just called, you have a room at the Hotel Utica for as long as you need it. There's a clothing store across the street, he says to just pick up what you need, he's called ahead."

The nurse handed Naomi a plastic bag that contained the sooty clothes she was admitted with.

"You also have a prescription for prenatal vitamins you can pick up at the nurse's station on your way out. It appears you've suffered no harm to the pregnancy."

TEA CUPS AND THE CLIFFS OF MOHER

A LETTER TO LILI-CHE FROM CHARLIE
ONE WEEK BEFORE THE SHOOTING IN JAMESTOWN

Che,

It is with extreme guilt and remorse that I write this. Guilt that I cannot tell you who I am, and remorse that our correspondence has turned you into my confessor and sin eater. I realize the things I tell you about what I have done are disturbing, and I am amazed you have the fortitude to respond to them. But there is something about you Che, something that compels me to tell you these things, these episodes of revenge and greed and violence that I have fallen in love with. Please know they all pale in comparison to the love I have for you. Please know I want to be the person you knew so many years ago.

It is for these reasons I have decided to take the chance, to put my trepidations to the side, and to arrange our meeting in the sincere hope you will remember me and how you once felt about me. I am truly ashamed of what I have evolved into, but I will turn that shame into resolve, I will be the man you deserve.

Please come visit me in Ireland, and please bring Sofia. I've enclosed your itinerary, the necessary arrangements and accommodations are set for two weeks from the receipt of this letter. There is a lovely village in the south of Ireland called Adare. It's quite rustic, with cobble stone streets lined with small cottages topped with thatched roofs. There is a beautiful Catholic Church there and across the street is a very old cemetery with limestone grave markers which are weathered beyond legibility. I like to sit there on my visits. I try to limit my business to a phone call or two while on these trips. My grandfather, my mom's dad, was born and raised here before moving northward.

He died long before I was born, and all I know of him was related to me by old timers who would fill me in on the details when they discovered I was Billy O'Malley's grandson. My grandfather spent some time in a British prison before his deportation to America and he was proud of it. He had some friends stateside who all felt betrayed by a controversial revolutionary whom they followed with blind devotion. Billy felt the same. When you kill for someone, for a cause you truly believe, everything that does not fit that cause is a betrayal. Like the others, Billy melded into another culture, an ocean away, but his anger and quest for revenge would never fade.

My mother rarely spoke of him, only to reminisce about his beautiful voice and the wonderful stories he would tell her of Ireland and his youth. But, in the same breath, she would condemn his drinking and temper. When my mother wasn't present, my father related a different picture of Billy. A portrait of an anarchist who would get into frequent fights at the railroad shops, swinging a pipe wrench at anyone who disagreed with him on England's oppression of Ireland.

Before our country entered the war, Nazi prisoners were shipped to prison camps in Canada via the rail line which ran through our city. When the train stopped to refuel, Billy would be there with baskets of sandwiches to pass out to the prisoners, urging them to escape and to kill Englishmen. He even fomented a riot when the local order of the Klan was going to stage a cross burning in the park on Madison Avenue. A Catholic was running for governor, so the Klan decided to focus on that and give people of color a break for a while. Billy and a gang of supporters, including a Catholic priest and nearly every Irishman in town, waded into the ceremony with axe handles and tire irons. It turned into a bloody blur of fists and clubs and knives. My father was a kid at the time, and he said next to the war, it was the most brutal thing he had ever witnessed. Coming from the least compassionate man I have ever known, that's saying something.

The first time I visited Adare, I had an uncanny feeling of being there before. Maybe it was knowing it was Billy's home that tied me to that strong sense of déjà vu, or maybe it was the dreams I had as a child, dreams of living in a cottage near a wooded area, staring at fish from a small footbridge which spanned a small brook, and being called back home by a beautiful woman with a blaze of red hair. Those dreams seemed so real and peaceful, I experience them again every time I visit.

We'll stay at Castle Adare, it's a hotel now. It's rich in architecture and history and it's haunted. Better not tell Sofia that, I wouldn't want to scare her. On bank holidays, I arrange for a carnival to set up between the castle and the cemetery. The children love the rides and games, especially the tea cup ride. What is it about the tea cup ride children cannot get enough of? Maybe it's because it's just scary enough to be fun. The carnival will arrive during our stay, I wouldn't want to deprive Sofia of that experience.

Before you leave, we'll head further south and walk the Cliffs of Moher. The trail provides a gorgeous view of the ocean along with gale force winds which never abate. Hold tight to Sofia or she might fly away. I guarantee you'll love the scenery and the people. There is a sense of calm here that can't be replicated anywhere else.

Once again I have poured my memories out to you, as if you are a muse, or the conscience I never had. I feel you are both, and I feel you will make me whole again, you will reshape me into someone with a benevolent sense of purpose and genuine empathy. And for that I will forever be in your debt.

The dates I've arranged are the only opportunity we'll have to meet before I get back to unfinished business. I'll be arriving in Ireland to meet you on my way back from Ukraine. Please say you'll come with Sofia, and be sure to bring your coats.

Love Always,
Gabriel

THE CARETAKERS

A HUNTING CABIN
MASSENA, NY
FEBRUARY 1967

Bertha Lipschitz and Virginia Crosby had blackmailed Father Cregan into meeting them at the hunting cabin. It had been a long drive from Utica to the cabin in bitter, below zero temperatures, and the priest was unaware of who he would meet, but the information he had received was disturbing.

The threat of jail time was not something he could ignore. For over twenty years his priesthood had been riddled with accusations of child abuse and molestation. The worst kind of accusations, the ugliest kind. He would not be moved to another parish this time, he would not be hidden, he could very well end up in prison.

He brought the money with him as instructed in the note, but he knew the blackmail would not stop as long as he had a nickel to his name, so in the gym bag along with the cash, he brought a pistol. The harassment was going to end one way or another.

The threats began a few weeks earlier, they came by mail and they were explicit in their detail, and the details were accurate and structured in the form of an indictment. He was ordered to cease his activities at once, which he did, but how did the blackmailers get this information, his victim had been warned what would happen, his victim was wrought with fear, it had to be someone else at the school, a busy body, someone with nothing better to do than snoop. He would take care of that busy body after settling the score with the blackmailers. This conspiracy needed to be brought to an end through any means necessary.

Bertha and Virginia exited the cabin and hid in the pine trees nearby when they saw the faint glimmer of headlights creeping down the long dirt road leading to the cabin. There was a full moon overhead illuminating a starry night sky. Their every breath was frozen in the night air. This part of the state was notorious for frigid temperatures during winter, but also noted for the lack of snow that accompanied those temperatures. The road was almost bare with the exception of a few patches of ice formed in the crevices of tire ruts.

"You look like Elmer Fudd, the way you're dressed," Bertha chuckled.

"These get-ups were your idea, I can't take this cold much longer, we need to get this over with."

Virginia shivered and pulled the ski mask over her head making sure the eyes and mouth were in position. Bertha did the same.

"Yes we do, but remember, once we get him in the cabin there's no turning back."

Father Cregan parked his car next to the vehicle already there and took careful note of the license plate. The letters had been smeared with clumps of frozen mud, a crude attempt to disguise them. He was to hand the bag to the driver of the vehicle, but the vehicle wasn't running, there was no one inside. A light shone from the cabin and the door was ajar, he could smell the wood smoke from the chimney as he turned to identify the sound behind him.

Out of the pine trees emerged Bertha and Virginia, wearing plaid hunting jackets and pants, accented by knee high boots, their faces hidden by the ski masks. Two middle aged women almost comical in their appearance except for the double barrel shotgun now pointed at the pedophile priest.

Bertha held the shotgun and motioned for Father Cregan to drop the bag he carried and to move up the stairs and into the cabin. Virginia examined the contents of the bag and threw the pistol into the nearby woods. She carried the gym bag with her into the cabin while Bertha motioned for the priest to be seated in a wooden kitchen chair next to the woodstove.

Bertha pressed the icy cold barrel of the shotgun against the priest's forehead while Virginia wrapped a logging chain around his wrists and ankles, and finally to the rear of the chair, securing it with a combination lock. The chain was heavy and Virginia's breathing deepened with each manipulation of the chain.

Now that their captive was secured, they removed their ski masks. Bertha stuffed the money the priest brought into the woodstove, she would discard the bag on the way home.

"So it's you two bitches, it makes sense now why we hired a Jew for a school nurse, you got your girlfriend in didn't you Virginia – you dykes make me sick, you're every bit as bad as me."

Virginia pulled up a kitchen chair and seated herself, still out of breath from wrapping the chain around the prisoner.

"You know what makes me sick, a pedophile priest, preying on little boys and threatening to send them to hell along with their families if they ever tell, that's what makes me sick."

Bertha warmed her hands above the woodstove before addressing Father Cregan.

"In addition to being a lesbian, I am a very competent nurse, and a dental hygienist, you got a bargain with me, Jew or no Jew."

"Just let me go and I'll get so far away from St. Anthony's you'll never see me again, it's a sickness you know, I'll check into a mental hospital….."

"So the Bishop can move you to a new parish, to prey on more kids, that's not going to happen this time."

Bertha cut off his attempt at a bargain mid-sentence.

Virginia motioned to Bertha who now stood behind the priest. She removed a hypodermic from her coat pocket and held it at the ready, just short of the side of the priest's neck, just out of his eyesight.

"You were flying under the radar until Tony DiFabio talked to us about the Bean kid, he had his suspicions, and then the kid opened up about it to Bertha, threats or no threats."

The priest was indignant, his ruddy cheeks now a bright red, in contrast with his thin, grey hair, combed from ear top to ear top to disguise his balding head. So it was a maintenance man who put all of this in motion.

"Go to hell you bitch," he screamed at Virginia.

"Give my regards to Satan, Father.

Virginia looked away as Bertha injected the contents of the hypodermic into the prisoner's neck. She did so without hesitation, and then bent to speak directly into the priest's ear, she wanted him to hear what she had to say before he slipped into unconsciousness.

"Well Father, when they find you in a few days, you'll be on the side of the road you drove in on, you will be face down and you will be dressed in your underwear, nothing else, and in your car a few yards away will be the suicide note describing how you planned it, everything from the narcotics in your blood stream to your plan to take a long walk in the woods on a frigid winter evening so you could die a painless death from exposure, because at the root of all of this, you are nothing but a coward devoid of soul or conscience."

The priest could no longer form words. His body went limp. Bertha pressed two fingers against his neck to check on a pulse. She wiped a small drop of blood from his neck with her other hand, the gloved hand. No obvious sign of the injection remained.

"He's still got a pulse, but it's slow and thready, we better get him undressed and out of here in a hurry, we don't need any signs of dermal blood pooling on him until we toss him in the ditch, it's got to look like he froze to death in the ditch."

They unchained him and undressed him. Next, they carried him down the cabin steps and loaded him into the trunk of his car and drove to the agreed upon spot down the driveway to deposit the body. The priest wasn't a large man, but the duo had never experienced carrying an unconscious adult before, and it was laborious. The typewritten suicide note and his clothes were meticulously arranged in his car. Bertha had forged his signature to the note after two weeks of practice.

Virginia's family had owned the cabin for decades, but after the death of her uncle, the deed holder, it had been unused for several years. No one else in the family wanted it, but Virginia still had a key. It was in a remote location, a mere stone's throw from Canada, and in poor repair. It just wasn't worth the effort for the next generation to restore it to its former beauty. It was to be sold for taxes in the coming spring.

The long walk back to the cabin was tolerable due only to the adrenalin coursing through the two assassins' bodies. Virginia was exhausted, but Bertha took her by the arm and pulled her along.

"Let's lock this place up – we've got time to double check everything, make sure we haven't left anything behind."

Bertha scanned the cabin from the doorway as Virginia seated herself once again in the kitchen chair.

Bertha's mind was racing as she verbalized what needed to be done before they made their escape. If they were to be caught it would be because of a detail, something forgotten in the fog of the moment, something minute, something thought to be insignificant. It's always the little things.

Virginia was of no use, she struggled to catch her breath before attempting any more physical exertion.

Bertha returned the shotgun to the rack on the wall and then shut the damper on the wood stove, snuffing out the remains of the fire. Only ashes remained in the hearth. She raced to the car and started it, the headlights beamed through the open front door. The logging chain and lock were deposited in the car trunk. She returned to the cabin where she extinguished the two kerosene lamps which sat on the kitchen table and pulled Virginia to her feet from the chair, and led her to the car.

"The ground's so frozen, I doubt they'll be able to notice any difference in tire tracks, but just to be sure, we'll get your tires changed Ginny, we have time, I'm betting they won't find him for days."

Virginia ducked her head in shame as their vehicle passed by the body in the ditch. Bertha stopped the car a few miles away from the crime scene. She exited the car for a moment and threw the gym bag from the shoulder of the road into a small culvert. She glanced at Virginia before putting the vehicle back into gear.

"What's wrong?"

"He had a pistol, I threw it into the woods."

There was panic in Virginia's voice.

"You did what?"

"I threw it into the woods, it scared me."

"Oh boy, we better hope they don't find that."

Bertha grimaced and slapped the steering wheel.

"It still won't link us to this, it was his gun."

"I hope you're right Bertha, I'm getting sick to my stomach."

"Relax, we just have to get these clothes to Good Will and the chain back in the garage and we're home free."

They drove in silence for the next hour before speaking of the evening's events. Bertha initiated the conversation.

"That poor Bean kid, I love it when he fakes being sick so he can come to see me, he's so funny, I don't think I've ever completed any of his fluoride treatments once he starts with his stories, I just love to hear them."

"There's a better than average chance he's mentally ill, there's been some issues with that family in the past."

"That's too bad, and that Cossack kid and that Gregory kid, I'll kiss your ass if they're not brothers somehow."

"Bertha, do you have to be so crude."

"I mean it Ginny, look at those two, don't tell me everything's not relative in this town, other mother brothers, that's what they are, daddy must've been busy."

Virginia laughed along with Bertha.

"If you know what's good for you Bertha, you won't say that to the Cossack kid's mother, she nearly killed someone at the grocery store with a can of soup because they bumped into her cart."

"No, really?"

"Really, she comes from a long line of Irish lunatics and the father's not much better, his family was run out of Europe by the Russians before the war, a bunch of rabble rousers, they wound up changing their name because of it."

"Now that's interesting….."

Bertha noticed the look on Virginia's face, a look of remorse.

"Don't do it Ginny, don't feel sorry for that son-of-a-bitch, if you could've seen what I saw in Poland during the war when I was a kid, you'd know his type wouldn't stop, they never do."

"So we should feel good about being judge, jury, and executioner?"

"Yes, and I'll tell you why, justice delayed is justice denied, we saved that poor kid, and others, from years of abuse at the hands of that sadist, I've seen his type before, they are without conscience, they are evil incarnate, they are empty drums."

"It all seemed so necessary, but now I'm thinking of other alternatives, other solutions...."

"Don't bother, those kids are like our children, what would any mother do to protect her children – they'd do what we did, you know that."

"I guess you're right, he would've been moved somewhere else, to start over again."

"You know what Ginny, we should buy that cabin and renovate it, wouldn't that be fun, you know, electricity and running water, we could retire there, free to be who we are."

"After tonight, you want to go back to that place – you must be out of your mind."

"Think about it, but right now you better hope we've got enough gas to get home, I don't want to fill this thing up dressed like I am."

"I just noticed something Bertha, your pants and coat don't match, different patterns of plaid, and before you move to the forest, you better learn how to load a shotgun, there's bears in them there woods."

Bertha looked down at the gas gauge. More than enough to get home. Soon, tonight would be just an unspoken memory. She smiled and took a quick glance at Virginia before returning her eyes to the road.

"Very funny Annie Oakley, very funny."

A PANOPLY OF FAT MEN (THE MUSICAL)

THE CUFFS AND COLLARS CLUB
JAMESTOWN, NY
1989

Charlie Cossack crawled underneath the limo after the shots rang out. From his vantage point there he could see blood pooling around the lifeless body of Gennady, a gentle rain was forcing a trickle of it underneath the limo. Charlie covered his wounded hip with his hand, afraid to look at what the damage was. Gennady had spotted the vehicle speeding by, a pick-up truck with two Asian men crouched in the bed, rifles against their shoulders. He pushed Charlie behind him and intercepted two rounds meant for his boss. Loyal to the end.

Charlie could hear some screams coming from the doorway of the club. Sirens echoed in the distance before he drifted in and out of consciousness, before the musical began, before he sat in the audience and witnessed a panoply of fat men who danced and sang to the rock and roll songs Charlie had listened to non-stop as a teenager.

But he knew these fat men, they were the mayors and city managers he had been conning for the better part of two years, a brilliant grift concocted by a Filipino politician and opportunist named Tommy Bocobo.

"What is it about you Americans, so many fat guys, and they almost all have moustaches, and they all have egos bigger than their waistlines."

Tommy would often opine about the men he and Charlie were conning. Tommy presented himself as an investor, an entrepreneur, seeking new investments for his wealthy employer headquartered in Manila. A giant pile of lies, but the fat guys ate it up as if they were devouring the calorie laden desserts they were addicted to. They must have known they were lies, but they were just too delicious not to eat.

Small city mayors, city managers, industrial development gurus, all trying to save their communities from the exodus of businesses, industries, and population. Times were tough, the urban dream was becoming a nightmare, interest rates soared and wages plummeted.

Tommy and Charlie would meet with these men to cajole investments and trust, but it didn't take much cajoling. The duo promised to build factories, and housing for the influx of workers, and it would be magical, communities would be transformed once again into the post-war economic utopia everyone wanted. And all it would take would be for these men to sign the checks over, over from the accounts of community development funds and industrial development grants.

In a sign of good faith, Charlie and Tommy promised to match the funding, but their shell companies were always liquidated after an abrupt bankruptcy filing. The ensuing bankruptcies all presided over by Charlie's attorney, Bonita Romero. Money only flowed in one direction, down a super highway that dead ended with Tommy and Charlie.

An intricate shell game of buying materials, replacing the materials with junk, over insuring the junk materials and then destroying them by any disaster possible, collecting the insurance money, and then reselling the genuine materials. It was a beautiful manipulation of hearts and minds, with Bonita controlling every pen-stroke of the scheme.

"And did you notice, these fat guys with their moustaches, they cackle when they laugh, but the biggest assholes are the ones wearing bow ties, now I ask you, what kind of idiot still wears a bow tie today?"

Another observation from Tommy delivered with glee, his enjoyment at duping his prey was no secret.

"And they're all too embarrassed to admit they've been conned, too afraid they'll go to jail with us, just big blobs of quivering jello."

Some did initiate lawsuits, but they were told it would take years before they saw a dime, legions of attorneys would need to wade through the mire of bankrupt shell companies and offshore accounts, and that in itself was a bigger financial threat than the con. It was a brilliant grift that bordered upon wizardry.

Ah yes, Charlie could see them now, the fat guys were on stage and they were twisting the night away, a chorus line of obesity, a conga line of blubber, and they all had moustaches, all types of moustaches, handlebar moustaches, pencil thin moustaches, Hitler moustaches, some of those moustaches were waxed, others covered the fat guys' mouths like the hair on a sheep dog covers its eyes. And they all wore ties, short ties, long ties, but those in the front of the chorus line all wore bow ties, bright, oversized bow ties.

"Dance fat boys, dance," Charlie mumbled as he was loaded onto the helicopter in preparation for the flight to the trauma center in Buffalo.

And they continued to dance, so light on their feet for obese men, but they sweated buckets, and one by one they began to drop, and the audience gasped, the audience screamed for them to get back on their feet, those tiny feet which ambulated those large bodies.

"Get back on your feet you fat bastards," someone in the audience heckled.

Those in attendance shook their fists and screamed at the fat guys, and those fat guys still standing began to cry, some fell to their knees and sobbed, others held their faces with sausage sized fingers and ran off the stage, and then Charlie catapulted into reality.

There were no fat guys in the room, no fat guys surrounding the hospital bed Charlie was in. Naomi Clearwater, a bartender at Charlie's pub in Buffalo sat in a nearby chair weeping. It had become obvious in the last few weeks that she was pregnant, and Gennady was the father. To her side and gently patting her back was Charlie's remaining body man, Bohdan.

Bohdan stepped to Charlie's bedside and spoke just loud enough for Charlie to hear.

"Bonita,she dead, overdose they say."

Charlie answered back, his voice hoarse and weak, but his eyes were now wide open.

"It was Roman, I want him dead, no more fucking around."

"Cops say Asian guys, probably Bocobo's guys."

"That's what Roman wants us to think, kill that son-of-a-bitch, and do it before they come for me here, no excuses, make it ugly."

Bohdan straightened his glasses, filthy from his fingerprints, and turned and left the room.

"Naomi, I'll get you to a safe place, it'll be alright…"

"Fuck you Charlie, fuck you all to hell," Naomi interrupted.

DAGGER UNDONE

THE PORT OF SAN FRANCISCO
1990

Dagger Lorow was prepared for surgery in an abandoned warehouse. The warehouse had been converted into a surgical suite in just days after Dagger received the news he had been matched for a kidney transplant. The news was delivered to him through an intermediary for his long time friend and business partner Charlie Cossack.

Since Charlie's disappearance close to a year ago, messages from him were delivered to the necessary confidantes through Bertha Lipschitz, a former nurse and dental hygienist where Dagger and Charlie had attended school. How that relationship was formed or the intricacies surrounding it were a mystery to all, including Dagger. Bertha was a petite woman, and as sarcastic as she was pleasant, and the students at St. Anthony's always referred to her as the "human lie detector."

The donor, a young Filipino man, was to receive enough cash to make him and his impoverished family comfortable for the rest of their lives. This cash was to flow from Charlie to the donor via another intermediary, a Filipino politician and racketeer named Tommy Bocobo.

Tommy had agreed to the arrangements in his usual style, a style steeped in cruel, outrageous humor.

"Who the hell do you think I am, Dr. Frankenstein?"

The phone call with Charlie was no exception.

"I'll double your usual fee and I'll take care of the donor's family for life, he just doesn't have time to wait for a kidney any other way, and remember, thanks to me, that maniac in Toronto is out of the picture, after me he was coming for you."

"Yeah, yeah, I'll get Igor on it right away, you fucking Americans think you can buy anything, even body parts."

And Tommy did find a donor as he had done so many times. It was not difficult to do in a country where people were so poor they would have traded a kidney for a color television. His foray into merchandising vital organs to the wealthy from the poor had been profitable. He even supplied the surgeons and equipment for the right price.

But being poor never made anyone stupid or less ambitious, rather just the opposite. Within Tommy's empire, he had discovered artisans and metal workers beyond compare. One of his first ventures was to duplicate hand guns, all forged within primitive metal huts in the more rural area of the Philippines. Just bring the actual model to them, and then supply them with the raw materials and it was done. A perfect working replica. And printing money was not a problem after the plates arrived from North Korea, and the paper from a mill in India. The ink manufactured in a small island village a few miles south of Manila.

Just fifty dollar bills, the most difficult to duplicate and the most tedious to move, but that was Charlie's responsibility, since he paid for them at one third their face value and willingly accepted them as payment for his movement of drugs and weapons to and through third world nations.

The hand guns and phony cash were moved into the United States through California and under the auspices of Dagger. He inspected each weapon and would report back to Charlie on their appearance and functionality. The counterfeit money was moved onward for distribution through another operative based on the Nevada border.

Dagger had become a prison guard for the California Bureau of Prisons in the years since leaving Utica. A day after graduating high school, Dagger hopped on his newly purchased motorcycle and set out on the trip of a lifetime, a cross country trek on his new bike.

"This is just something I have to do Charlie, when the money runs out I'll probably be back, I just don't feel comfortable here anymore."

This discomfort generated by a police interview about burglaries at local pharmacies. Dagger and Charlie had been breaking into drug stores with nothing more than a brick chisel and a sheet rock knife. The pharmacies they targeted were all in strip malls and of block construction. They could remove enough concrete blocks from the back of these stores in minutes to allow them to snake through. From the stock room they could gain entry into the pharmacy itself by simply cutting an opening into the sheetrock separation wall. Doors, which were alarmed, never needed to be pried.

Armed with a list of medications to be taken, they went to work with pen lights taped to their wrists. The list was created by Dagger's older sister who would ultimately move the drugs through a local dealer.

A few days before a robbery, Dagger would scope out the crime by using the rest room at the store to be targeted. Most of the time the rest rooms were located in the storage areas of the store. He'd get a good look at the wall separating the pharmacy from the stock room and any doors that were alarmed.

After the last job, an employee thought a young customer acted somewhat odd when he asked to use the rest room a day before the last burglary. She told the police about the mysterious customer and the motorcycle he rode after she followed him to the front door.

"I needed to take a piss, what the hell."

Dagger was indignant when the police questioned him on the front porch of his grandmother's house. His sister stayed inside, to the side of the door, listening for any slip ups her brother might make. He remained convincing and defiant throughout the questioning.

That evening, Dagger, and his sister Chloe, removed field stones from the basement foundation of their grandmother's house and tucked the maul, chisel, and sheetrock knife deep into the dirt along with a sealed plastic bag of cash before replacing the stones. The remaining plastic drug vials and bottles were mixed within bags of garbage, after being carefully checked for any identifiers, and wiped down, and disposed of the next day at the County landfill.

Chloe watched the loader, equipped with a grading blade, bury the evidence deep underground. When the police arrived with their warrant they found nothing. Dagger's grandmother, suffering from dementia, chased them from the front porch after they finished their search.

After his relocation to California, Dagger reached out to Charlie after securing the prison guard job. As was his habit, he studied the ins and outs of the system, exploring it for its weaknesses and strengths.

"The only difference is I get to go home at night," Dagger confessed to Charlie.

"You mail me any drug you get your hands on and I can move it through the prison, the guards already have a system to do it, but I'm gonna' fine tune it."

And that Dagger did with precision. Not only did drugs flow unabated into the prison where he worked, along with them came weapons and cash for protection and retaliation. Soon, prison after prison became part of the scheme, a spider web of endemic corruption. All of this financed by the gangs which had taken hold in the metropolitan centers of California.

"I'm not shitting you Charlie, every religion, every race, every group with a beef or some fucked up ideology has a gang here, and they all hate each other, and they pay good for every favor we do, keep sending the drugs."

Charlie lived up to his part of the bargain and the United States Postal Service was none the wiser. None the wiser until the DEA had discovered the use of drug sniffing dogs along the border and the Postal Service soon followed suit. But as soon as that avenue closed, vans and drivers were recruited and hired by Charlie's boss in Toronto to keep the commodity moving, from east coast to west coast and to any destinations in between.

About the time the supply chain had been smoothed out, Dagger made the acquaintance of a young Korean woman named Winnie Kwon. Winnie's family owned a chain of nail parlors, and Winnie managed them all. Her brother was doing a 20 year sentence for a gang related murder and Winnie reached out to the guards about some preferential treatment for him. Dagger agreed to her request, the only thing he asked for in return was that she receive packages from the Philippines at her businesses. Packed in the crates of nail polish and acetone were handguns and counterfeit money. Winnie would drive the bogus cash to operatives in Reno once a month while Dagger marketed the handguns. All of this accomplished by protecting and pampering Winnie's incarcerated brother.

And then the impossible happened. Dagger began to care for Winnie – her safety, her feelings, her feelings for fuck's sake, that was a new one, Dagger was not familiar with that emotion. They began to stockpile money in hopes of an escape, for they knew the enterprises they were entrenched in would someday result in a catastrophic collapse, a collapse resulting in long prison sentences. Charlie had managed to vanish, he promised he could help them do the same.

But then the wild card, kidney disease was taking a toll on Dagger, he would soon need a transplant to survive and he didn't have time to wait. It had to be soon and once the message got through to Charlie through his convoluted maze of contacts and messages, and phone booths, and cryptic classified ads, the plan took form.

Bertha, the linchpin of Charlie's opaque, yet efficient network of communications, was sent to oversee the transplant procedure in San Francisco. She had been an army nurse during the Korean War and was no stranger to operating room protocols.

"Keep your eyes open Bertha, I don't trust Bocobo as far as I can throw him."

Charlie's suspicions were shared by Bertha.

"I don't like him either, and I don't like the whole idea of this, the only reason I'll do it is for Dagger and I know you'll take care of the donor and his family."

"That's guaranteed Bertha, everyone will be taken care of, you know I never lied to you."

"And there's something else Charlie, I want Virginia moved to a bigger room, one large enough for me to stay in and take care of her."

"That won't be a problem, I'll get the wheels moving on that as soon as I hang up."

"And I want the Montana girl and her boyfriend Butler reunited, they've passed every drug test I've given them for over a year, and Virginia loves the poems the Montana girl has written when I read them to her, you need to have them published as well."

"You drive a hard bargain Bertha, but I'll make it happen, I promise, all of it will happen."

Virginia, Bertha's significant other, and a retired teacher from the school where they both worked, was now residing in a private nursing facility which still fell under the prevue of Charlie's management in abstentia. Charlie had always been close to Virginia, she had faith in him when his panic attacks were at their worst as a child. She had become the mother he always wanted.

The surgery failed before it started. Bertha sat in her car, parked across the street from the warehouse, and watched a group of federal agents surround the complex. Winnie was led out in handcuffs along with Dagger who was in a wheelchair. The transplant donor now wore a jacket marked with the letters "FBI."

A disappointed Charlie instructed Bertha to arrange bail for both Winnie and Dagger.

"Lorow has been moved to a dialysis center, but I put up the bond for the Kwon girl, she's been released, the charges are all about a transplant ring, nothing else."

The bondsman relayed the information to Bertha who in turn reached out to Charlie from a pay phone at the airport.

"It seems you were right about Bocobo, it looks like Dagger will die before he gets a transplant, prisoners come last."

"Bertha, get hold of Winnie and tell her not to do anything stupid, this isn't over yet."

"There's something else Charlie, one of those agents I saw, he looked really familiar, I think I've seen him in Utica before, maybe working at the nursing home, and I know this sounds stupid, but he looks like that boxer, George Foreman, you know who I mean, right?"

"That makes sense, Dagger said a big guy had been staking out the nail parlors – it's like you always said Bertha, we're all just one detail away from failure at any given moment."

The phone line went dead. Bertha stepped away from the bank of payphones and walked to her flight terminal, suitcase in hand. She'd give Winnie a call from another payphone when she switched flights in Chicago.

Thousands of miles and one continent away, Charlie Cossack limped to the window of his home and balanced himself upon a cane. He could see the aviaries from there. Three of them constructed for birds according to size. Small, medium, and large. Today was supposed to be a great day, Dagger would get his kidney, Lili-Che was on her way along with Bohdan and her daughter Sofia, and the orioles were due to arrive. But today was not going to be that day.

Charlie pulled a greeting card envelope from the pocket of the sweater he was wearing. It was folded and had been unopened since the day it was handed to him, nearly three years ago. It had been presented to him by a stranger riding a bicycle. The stranger, small in stature, was garbed in an aluminized hood, the type an airport firefighter would wear while battling a fuel fire. His hands were covered with the same material in what appeared to be elbow long mittens. He rode by Charlie on the sidewalk in front of the Bar & Grill in Utica. As Charlie stepped aside, he was handed the envelope.

Charlie, for some reason unknown to him, felt no urgency to open the envelope, no sense of curiosity as to its contents, he could not have cared less, and he didn't understand or care why he felt that way. Bonita Romero stood alongside him, she had asked to speak to him outside before the mysterious stranger presented his gift.

"So, what the hell is it, aren't you going to open it?"

"Who knows, but since the fire at the nursing home, we've had a bunch of weirdos showing up here, probably something to do with him, him or that bullshit about the white cardinal showing up there."

Charlie pocketed the envelope, still not understanding why he could not bring himself to open it.

But today, at the ranch, his feelings had changed, he felt an overwhelming urge to open the envelope. The urge had been building ever since Lili-Che had accepted his invitation to visit the ranch.

And so, while seated at the upstairs window from which the aviaries were visible, he tore the envelope open to find the gold cross he had purchased for her over 20 years ago. He had always wanted to believe she was wearing it the night of the accident, thinking of him on that Valentine's Day, but now, here it was, falling out of an envelope delivered to him by an eccentric courier three years ago. And for some reason, it all made sense now.

"Just get me near that son-of-a-bitch Bocobo, and I'll do the rest."

Chloe Lorow stepped in front of Charlie and stared out the window, her fists clenched, her voice punctuated with rage, an emotion Charlie was all too familiar with.

"I can arrange that, but you'll have to do something else, I promised Dagger I'd get Winnie out if things went sideways, can you promise me that?"

Chloe shook her head in agreement.

"If that's what he wants, then that's what I'll do, you know that."

THE TOOTHACHE

TORONTO, CANADA
1989

Roman Aranofsky was many things to many people. In Ukraine, as a youth, he exposed families who hid Jews during World War II. All for a pat on the head and a few pieces of chocolate from a Nazi officer. He bartered the chocolate away in return for favors. When the Nazis retreated, he pointed out collaborators to the advancing Russian army. All for a pat on the head and some tobacco and eggs which he used as currency to plot his escape westward. Sooner or later, he knew, someone would be pointing him out to another advancing army, or to a family seeking revenge.

Roman could speak many languages. Ukrainian, Polish, Russian, and Yiddish among them. This was not unusual or a sign of intelligence, only a hallmark of self preservation. Ukraine was a melting pot of languages, and at any given time Russia would ban a specific language to enforce its policy of Russification upon Ukraine. The penalty for speaking a forbidden language in public was often death. Roman would use those languages to transform himself into the ethnicity of his choosing whenever it served as an advantage. Each of those advantages achieved through new levels of stealth and betrayal.

Claiming to be a Jew brought him to the newly formed state of Israel. From there, claiming to be a persecuted Ukrainian national, he was allowed citizenship into Canada. Other branches of his family had been granted asylum in America. He kept track of them, for someday he may need to use them to his advantage, they could be exploited for his benefit. Manipulation had become an art form for Roman.

The other Aranofskys, those living in America, fearing retaliation from the Russian Communist Party, for they actually were Ukrainian nationalists, and had campaigned against communism, changed their last name. No sense in drawing attention to themselves. Their lineage was cluttered with poets and revolutionaries, all singing the praises of a free Ukraine. Portraits of these revolutionaries still hung in some American Aranofsky homes. However, the penalty for reciting an Aranofsky poem in Ukraine was still a swift and certain death.

After arriving in Toronto, Roman began recruiting other refugees from Eastern Europe under the promise of employment which they would repay with loyalty. His first job was in a laundry. Within a year he owned the laundry after the owner died under questionable circumstances, leaving Roman as the sole owner, a shock to the original owner's family. Afterwards, that family suffered a series of catastrophic events. Everything from drowning to house fires to motor vehicle accidents.

The laundry flourished under Roman. They delivered dry cleaning to homes and uniforms to businesses and hospitals in the greater Toronto area. They also delivered narcotics and weapons for the right price. Roman had become interested in a drug used by German soldiers during the war. It gave them energy, but the side effects were concerning. Weight loss, agitation, and confusion among them.

So, as was his desire to covet anything that interested him, Roman acquired the formula for this drug from a Nazi chemist he smuggled into Canada under the guise of starting a new life. He patented the formula and opened a chain of weight loss clinics targeting housewives. Housewives living the post-war dream. The dream of owning a home of their own, having children, caring for those children and a husband, while at the same time feeling distressed and unattractive from the weight gain of multiple pregnancies, and gasping for breath from under the crush of responsibilities the dream had thrust upon them.

A group of housewives could throw their children into the back of the station wagon and drive to the clinic for a weekly injection of the miracle drug. A simple and effective solution. And it worked so well, it was apparent, but so were the side effects, and so was the dependency it caused. The clinics soon bled across the border and into American cities, big and small. Hence, the methamphetamine crisis was born, years before it would be identified.

And then came the damage. Ill health, loss of teeth, frightening weight loss, and the never ending craving for more, more, more. It made the post-war dream livable, while at the same time ravaging the bodies and minds of unsuspecting women.

Roman took the bad news in stride. His miracle weight loss drug would need to be regulated by the government. The damage it caused was obvious, something needed to be done to stop the carnage it had inflicted.

Ever resourceful, Roman exited the manufacture of this drug, but he invested in some others, others that when subjected to acids and bases, would yield the miracle drug once again. These were simple drugs and legal, over the counter drugs, most of them antihistamines, and readily available. He would manufacture and warehouse these drugs and market them to those willing and able to transform them into what the public really wanted.

His most fervent customers were the biker gangs which had cropped up around the United States. Many of these were formed by disgruntled war veterans who had gotten a taste of the miracle drug in Europe. The Nazis weren't the only ones feeding it to soldiers.

These customers took the precursors and cooked them until they created their new product. They used the drug, they marketed the drug, and they kept it cost effective to compete with anything else being sold on the street. And they became wealthy from the drug, but not as wealthy as Roman who took his profits and branched out into other venues.

He could and would give the public anything they wanted, but were afraid to ask for. Pornography, prostitution, drugs, guns – political pressure and blackmail became his specialties, the more people in his pocket the better. And, being a true entrepreneur, he was always on the lookout for talent. But, today's talent could be tomorrow's downfall. He knew that full well. The addiction to his newfound brand of capitalism and commerce swallowed him whole, there was no turning back.

He assembled refugees, defectors, and asylum seekers, employed them, and used them to guarantee his safety and well being. Most of them hailed from Eastern Europe and were granted work visas through his many businesses. Those escaping from communist countries went to the front of the line when applying for citizenship during the cold war.

Two of the more interesting recruits had applied for asylum after arriving with the Moscow Circus in Toronto. They were large men. They wrestled bears, ripped phone books in half, and bent iron bars around their necks. During one point of the performance, audience members were offered a prize if they could wrestle one of the giants to the ground. It didn't matter how many rushed the arena, they would be rewarded if one of the giants was brought to the ground. Some in the audience tried, but they failed. They were tossed aside like dolls, the giants would take them by their arms and legs and launch them back into the crowd. It didn't take long for the rest of the audience to see the folly of their efforts.

Roman, like any villain or superhero, had a weakness. He had been overly concerned with his health for years. An abscessed tooth nearly took his life when he arrived in Israel. He spent a week in a hospital, the infection stopped just short of his brain. After that event, he scheduled monthly visits with a dentist and at one point even considered having all of his teeth removed to prevent any further infections. He was assured his monthly visits would be enough to stave off another infection.

His entourage would accompany him on these monthly visits. The reception room was cleared of patients and staff. Two body men would remain with the vehicle and two others would be stationed in the waiting room. The dentist, a former Nazi, and brought into Canada by Roman, was repeatedly threatened before any examination or treatment, of the consequences he would face if anything were to go wrong.

On the day of his last appointment, Roman arrived precisely on time, the waiting room had been cleared and his two guards seated themselves and began leafing through magazines. Roman positioned himself in the dentist's chair and lifted his chin to allow the dentist to wrap the gauze bib around his neck.

The dentist stepped back and Roman sensed a shadow blocking the examination light from his face. In seconds, two mammoth hands covered his face, from his neck to his mouth. The hands began to squeeze. The pain was intense, but Roman's screams for help were muffled beneath the massive hands which crushed his skull. The giant was in no hurry, the cracking of bones appeared to nauseate the dentist, he bent over in disgust.

The dentist, a thin, elderly man, raised his head to see the giant approach him. He remained silent out of fear. The giant wiped his bloodied hands on the dentist's white smock, and effortlessly snapped the dentist's neck.

The giant then took the coat tree adjacent to the examination room door and snapped it in half over his knee. He gave it a swing to test its weight and ease of movement. The door fell to the floor of the waiting room with one thunderous kick and the giant approached the two body men with weapon in hand.

SOFIE AND GOLIATH

THE JOURNEY TO PATAGONIA
1989

Lili-Che Faithful took a long, last look at her apartment building as the cab drove away. In the back seat with her and Sofia was a small travel bag as was instructed. Just a change of clothes, her medications and some things to keep Sofia busy on the journey. Movers had arrived an hour earlier to prepare the rest of her luggage and necessities for their next destination.

She had lived a Spartan lifestyle until Gabriel emerged from the shadows. She often wondered if it all wasn't some quirky fairy tale she had invented out of despair. There were so many unanswered questions, but still, she had convinced herself she must face the final chapter of this mystery, there would be no turning back now. She owed that to herself.

At times, the riddle surrounding her relationship with Gabriel, her mystery man, and mystery lover, appeared to crack. It was as if she had found the door, that once opened, would put to rest all of the uncertainty. Something, maybe an elusive memory, a wisp of a thought she could not comprehend, had been tearing apart her brain for years, ever since her discharge from the rehabilitation center in Albany.

The plane ride to Miami was uneventful. After staring out the window for an hour or so, Sofia had nodded off to sleep. Lili looked about the first class cabin and appreciated all the amenities. A stewardess offered her a drink and a blanket for Sofia. She accepted a bottle of water and had previously turned down the meal. She was much too nervous to eat. This whole process had been as scary as it was exciting. Who was this man she was traveling to meet. He didn't show when she traveled to meet him in Ireland, why should she think he would now. A burst of anger raced through her mind. It could all be some sort of gigantic hoax, perpetrated by some geriatric millionaire, someone she had met at the club. She could be someone's obsession, and not in a good way. As the plane landed she struggled to put those thoughts out of her mind. She had no reason not to believe what Gabriel had told her. She needed to cling to those thoughts.

She strode from the plane with her carry on in one hand, clutching Sofia's hand with the other. Sofia had been awakened and was not happy about it. She held her silk rabbit under her arm as they made their way to the terminal.

And there he was, a hulking beast who at first glance might have appeared lost or disoriented if not for the cardboard sign in his hand which read "Bohdan." Lili wondered why her name was not on the sign, but she walked towards him scanning the rest of the terminal for others who may be watching. Over the past two years she had succumbed to the feeling of being watched many times, but each time she convinced herself the watchers were just ordinary people, her fears unjustified.

"Hello, Lili," the giant mumbled.

"Hello, Bohdan."

Lili hoped she had pronounced his name correctly. There wasn't an inch of his sport coat or trousers that didn't appear wrinkled. He was wearing wing tips that were severely scuffed and polished in a haphazard fashion.

"Ya," Bohdan replied as he adjusted his glasses and tucked the sign under his arm. He took Lili's carry on from her hand and smiled at Sofia.

On the way to the next airport, the private airport, Bohdan would only nod his head in agreement to any of the questions Lili asked. The conversation soon evolved into a flood of questions from Sofia which Bohdan would respond to with "Ya, right," or "Ya, nice," or, "Ya, Sofie."

At times, Lili would muffle a giggle as Sofia's questions ran the gamut as only those of a curious seven year old could. One question led to another, and to another, but Bohdan didn't seem annoyed at the precocious child's interrogation. She would poke her head through the window separating the passenger compartment from the Goliath at the wheel and explore every new train of thought with a barrage of questions. Bohdan would fidget with his glasses and reply in very calm and polite two word answers.

"You've got something stuck in your moustache," Sofia noted.

Bohdan pulled a scrap of food from his moustache and examined it before flicking it to the floor.

"T'ank you Sofie."

It was a limousine with seating for six in the back, along with a bar, stereo system, and a sunroof. Sofia was busy searching for radio stations when not assaulting Bohdan with questions. It was close to an hour's drive to the smaller airport and Lili was feeling more enervated by the mile.

Once at the airfield, the three of them boarded a small, private jet as an attendant pulled the limousine away. Bohdan adjusted his glasses once again and motioned to the stairs, an overt attempt at graciousness.

They were greeted at the stairs by a slim young woman wearing a navy blue skirt and a lighter blue blouse. Pinned to the blouse, at shoulder level, was a broach, a white broach. She shook Lili's hand and knelt to greet Sofia eye to eye.

"We're so glad you could come visit Sofia."

There was an accent tied to her voice that Lili recognized as British, but she quickly remembered that Gabriel told her most of the residents at the ranch were of Welsh descent, and if they speak another language at times, it should be of no concern.

"I like your bird pin, it's pretty."

"We can get you one Sofia if you'd like."

Sofia smiled and shook her head.

Everything seemed to make sense at this point. Bohdan, the jet, a Welsh accent, but Lili felt the onset of another migraine approaching, creeping through the confusion which was always just one thought away.

After they boarded, Lili sat across from Bohdan who was still answering Sofia's rapid fire questions in his succinct way. The attendant asked Sofia if she would like to pick out a snack before the plane landed to refuel. The attendant came back with orange jello topped with whipped cream. Lili sat entrenched in thought, still trying to pull something from the deepest recesses of her brain, something, a thought or a memory, which could calm her uneasiness.

The pilot alerted everyone to buckle up as they were going to land in Panama for fuel. Again, as Gabriel had outlined in his letters, but Lili's apprehensions arrived in waves – fear followed by anger, followed by excitement.

The jet touched down at a remote landing field and a fuel truck drove to its side. Bohdan exited the plane and met with some men in military uniforms sitting in a jeep some yards away. Lili watched him present the soldiers with a valise. He was handed a cardboard box in return which he kept looking into on his way back to the plane. He kept looking and smiling.

Upon re-entering the plane he set the box down next to Sofia's seat. She had once again dozed off. Bohdan patted her on the head with his enormous hand. She opened her eyes and caught sight of the box and its contents.

"Sofie, this you puppy, Boris."

Sofia squealed with delight as the beagle puppy licked her face.

"He know tricks, he shake hands."

Bohdan was pleased with Sofia's reaction. A smile spread across his face.

Sofia was wide eyed for the rest of the journey. Boris sat, rolled over, sat, rolled over, and shook hands for the entirety of the flight. A few minutes before the plane landed, Bohdan presented Sofia with a leash and collar he helped attach.

After the plane taxied down the air strip, Lili noticed two vehicles approaching. Once again a limousine, this time followed by a golf cart. The limo driver parked the car and left in the accompanying golf cart.

Bohdan walked his passengers to the limo and opened the door for them. Boris was jumping about as Lili looked out the window. There were some structures off in the distance. As they drew closer, the structures appeared to be what Gabriel had told Lili, an entire community secluded in this beautiful wonderland.

They drove under a wrought iron arch with the name "White Cardinal Ranch," displayed on it. In the distance she could see some corrals and sheep dotting the country side. This was all as Gabriel had described, but how could this be, she wondered, how could this be happening to her.

"Hey Sofie, you like birds?"

Bohdan was pointing to the aviaries. Three huge structures separated by smaller stone structures in between. They were as large as football fields and the netting was all of two stories high. Lili suddenly realized the smears on the shoulders of Bohdan's coat were bird droppings. He must spend time in the aviaries when he's not spreading mayhem around the world for his boss.

"Hey Sofie, you like tea cup ride?"

Bohdan pointed towards his right as the limo inched by a small amusement park."

"Boss say they running tonight after fireworks, boom, boom, boom."

"Look at that mom," Sofie squealed, "just like Ireland."

Lili sat in silence. She felt the onset of another migraine. How could this be real, how can any of this be real. Upon arrival at the main structure, the estate as Gabriel had referred to it, Bohdan led them up the stone staircase to the main entrance. The house was massive and built from stone and huge timbers, all topped with a terra cotta roof. A castle in the style of a Swiss chalet. They were greeted at the double doors by an elderly gentleman dressed in a pin striped business suit.

He led them in silence to a den just off the foyer. Clad in hardwood and lined with book shelves, the room had the feel and odor of a library. Lili had always found a sense of peace in libraries. Surrounded by stories, and science, and history, Lili had always felt comforted by being within their walls. There was one notable difference. This library had pool tables. Six of them arranged on the horizontal plane of the room. Just before the tables was a small desk, centered in the room. The only light in the room came from the fixtures above the pool tables, and one solitary desk lamp. The curtains were drawn on the windows. The older gentleman motioned her to the desk and then exited along with Bohdan, closing the oak double doors behind them.

The only items on the desk besides the lamp, was another letter, opened, the pages uncreased, and a small gold cross and chain upon it. Lili sat at the desk as Sofia chased her puppy around the room, stopping intermittently to allow the dog to do his tricks.

Lili held the cross and chain in her hand and read the letter. She closed her eyes and took a slow, deep, breath.

CONSUMMATION

As my affinity for you grows, I am compelled to share something, something fascinating. But I warn you, fascination is most often wrapped in danger.

If you wish to join me, you'll have to suspend reality for a few moments, for if you don't, I fear you may be devoured by an all-consuming angst. I will create a new reality for you, a reality where up is down and down is up, a reality where colors are distinguished by taste and not sight, a reality where emotions manifest themselves as waves of odor, some pungent, some sweet.

Walk with me now, towards a murky wasteland where universes collide. There is an intersection in this dystopia where philosophy, religion, and science meld into one another. Physicists and astronomers race from telescope to telescope, hoping to see the face of God. Mathematicians build pyramids, but just as quickly as they are completed, nihilists tear them down. Clerics and philosophers are locked in eternal warfare, a carnage that never achieves a goal, it serves only to invigorate more hate and violence.

Ignore this chaos and walk with me, the fog is lifting in the distance and this is where we must go. I have built something beautiful here you must experience to understand. Come closer and stand with me upon a hill crest overlooking a small valley. Below us I have constructed a drive-in theater, but no ordinary one. The screen is massive, beyond description, and the field adjacent to it is satiated with every make and model of vehicle.

It is a cool night late in the summer. Vehicle windows are steamed over with the passions of young lovers while children sprint back and forth between the playground and their parents. The swings are popular here, they take you as high as you wish – children can touch the clouds surrounding a blood red moon. They long to jump, but they never do.

The concession stand serves up memories, the good and the bad, the savory and the sour. There is a parade of customers that never abates, single file and anxious, they get what they asked for from an angry, balding woman with a cigarette perched in the corner of her mouth. Above her head is a sign patched together with removable letters. It simply states, "Live in the moment, not the past."

Please, have a seat on the couch behind us. An ocean of serenity engulfs you as I motion towards the screen, your fears now replaced with curiosity. We're showing clips from your life tonight, it's your choice, anything you want – love, hate, revenge, compassion, it's all here. Relive your first kiss, the death of a loved one, the birth of your child, your birth, the devotion of a lover, a spouse's betrayal, it's all just one thought away. You might find it interesting to experience these memories through the eyes of others, friends and enemies alike. Crawl inside them and take a peek.

This is overwhelming as well as addictive, and I'm concerned you've had enough for one visit. Let my creation dissolve now. Let go. You have a life to return to with all the responsibilities it brings, and you'll soon realize the moments you spent in my creation were actually hours in your reality.

I can bring you here again, but there is a catch. Isn't there always a catch? You must thaw my frozen soul with your thoughts and words, you must make me yearn to think and feel – make me a child again, leaping down the stairs on Christmas morning, my heart bursting with anticipation. Fill my soul with your spirit and imagination and I will have found redemption. Do so and I will swear my fidelity to you.

###

Remember, it's not about where you start; it's all about where you finish.

CHARLIE COSSACK'S BAR AND GRILL

40197371R00156